Frances Mary Peard

The Country Cousin

Vol. 2

Frances Mary Peard

The Country Cousin
Vol. 2

ISBN/EAN: 9783337231422

Printed in Europe, USA, Canada, Australia, Japan

Cover: Foto ©Andreas Hilbeck / pixelio.de

More available books at **www.hansebooks.com**

BY

FRANCES MARY PEARD

AUTHOR OF

'THE ROSE GARDEN,' 'CONTRADICTIONS,' 'ALICIA TENNANT,'
'HIS COUSIN BETTY,' ETC.

IN THREE VOLUMES

VOL. II.

LONDON

RICHARD BENTLEY AND SON

Publishers in Ordinary to Her Majesty the Queen

1889

THE COUNTRY COUSIN.

CHAPTER XIV.

TRUE to his resolve, Lancaster went down to Ashbury the next day, although it cost him much inconvenience. He was directed to the village from the station, and presently found himself on a gravelly road which ran like a yellow streak along the common. The broken ground was full of beauty, sheltered to the left by a closely grown belt of fir-trees, their somewhat sombre colouring here and there relieved by a solitary beech. These trees, however, merely edged a portion of the common, and stopped abruptly, leaving it to

sweep upwards until it reached the open
space where the windmill stood, a landmark
for miles around. The road turned away
long before this was even approached, and
ran downhill, the common to the right falling
still more steeply and losing itself in boggy
tracts of cotton rush, beyond which a cottage
or two became visible, and a pretty wood
clambered up another hill. Here in this little
green nest lay the cottage to which Lancaster
had been directed, but he paused on his way
to it, catching sight of red chimneys a little
to the left, peeping up above trees. He
knew very well that this must be Joan's home,
and his desire to see it drew him on one side
and through an iron gate, flanked by a lodge.

He walked up the drive and to the door,
but he would not go in. A gardener touched
his hat, and he explained briefly that he was
a friend of Lord Medhurst's, and had just
looked in to see the garden. This the man
took as a personal compliment, and showed

his gratification by an inclination to stand and talk, which Lancaster endured more patiently than would otherwise have been the case, from the hope that Joan's name, some little trait of his love, might slip into his hearing. It did not come, and he cast forth a feeler.

'Does Miss Medhurst take much interest in your work?'

'Oh, ay, sir; when it's flowers to be gathered. But she'd sooner be about with the dogs or down in the village, any day. You're not seeing it at its best, sir; for when his lordship's home he's that particular, we mustn't have a stray leaf about the place; but when he's away the boys take advantage.'

'And you've lost your poor old helper, the old woman who weeded, haven't you?'

'Old Martha, sir? Yes, poor old soul, it's a bad job for her; but as for helping, it's only to please her ladyship that she's let to potter about, and pick up a bit of a weed here and

there, where she can find it. A woman's
better anywhere than in a garden, to my
thinking.'

This, to a man whose mind was full of one
woman, was unsympathetic enough to cause
Lancaster to dismiss Mr. Andrews, and to
stand awhile alone looking at the closely
trimmed lawn, about which, in truth, only
lingered the impression of Lord Medhurst's
accurate individuality, and to try to picture
the young girl standing like a nymph in the
foreground. There was a fine copper beech,
which, in all its freshness of young leaf, made
a very complete setting for this picture.

He turned at last and walked quickly away.
His face had lost its occasional sternness, and
there was a very kindly look in his eyes.
Hardly anyone who came across this man
could fail to acknowledge the strong forces of
his nature—his dominant will, his concentra-
tion of purpose, his almost scornful rectitude.
But there were not many who guessed what

tenderness lay beside the strength, ready to spring up at a touch. The touch had come, and the tenderness answered it. All his thoughts of Joan were possessed by it, and his love seemed to him something sacred and wonderful—something which he had read of, but had never tasted for himself.

He passed out of the gates, and made his way down the hill towards the scattered cottages, which were only an offshoot from the village, and lay at some distance from the church. An excited family of geese were crossing the broken common to the right, and hurrying with outstretched necks across the road. Smoke curled upwards against the blue distance ; a nightingale was singing in the wood. Lancaster found the Potters' cottage, pushed open a small wooden gate, and walked up a path paved with round stones, between borders which it was not difficult to guess were supplied with flowers from the Manor, and which were backed with

gooseberry-bushes. Lancaster had knocked
at the door, and a voice had bidden him
' Come in,' before he was seized with an un-
familiar discomposure at his want of acquaintance with the class of people he had come to
see. The poor, however, seldom show surprise, and a rather slatternly young woman—
who could only be supposed by a stretch of
courtesy to be putting the kitchen to rights—
asked him to walk upstairs, where were both
husband and wife lying in their helplessness.
Martha turned her eyes wearily towards the
new-comer, under whose heavy tread stairs
and flooring creaked protestingly, but
Thomas's look brightened.

' Miss Medhurst wanted to know how you
were, and whether you had all that the doctor
ordered, and so I have come to find out,' said
Lancaster in a kindly voice.

' Bad, bad enough,' the old woman
answered quaveringly. ' 'Tis a bad job for
us, with Thomas lying like a log, and what-

ever he'll do when he haven't got me to look after him, Oi can't say, Oi'm sure.'

Thomas, who had a thin wiry face, with keen eyes, made a movement of his head towards his wife.

'Her'll have to get used to it, sir,' he said cheerfully. ''Tis all strange to her being shut up in four walls, and her's pretty well mazed to think the sun should get up of a morning when her can't. But Oi tell her when her's a lain here a matter of voive or six years, that'll pass.'

'There, sir, that's what he goes on a-saying,' Martha said with some pardonable bitterness. 'He's allays a-throwing up at me that Oi've got to lie here along of he, and me that's niver known a day's illness, and allays kept him clean and comforrable. But he'll voind the difference, poor soul, bymeby.'

'Who have you got to look after you?' asked Lancaster. 'I shall see Miss Med-hurst to-morrow, and she will want to hear everything. She is very much grieved at your accident.'

'Well, sir, if you'll please to tell her that Rose Turner comes in and does what she can ; but she's a poor hand, and when Oi get about again, there'll be a deal o' putting to rights. And Mrs. Jones sends down beef-tea, and that doos for Thomas, for Oi don't stomach anything much. Just pick a bit o' what comes handy. Oh, my poor leg!'

'The doctor don't think very well of her,' said Thomas.

'No,' said Martha, accepting this view as a fitting tribute, and wiping her eyes. 'And there's the shrubbery—no one 'll see to the weeds. Mr. Andrews, he may be a grand gardener, but he haven't no conscience about the weeds ; he just turns 'em over, and digs 'em in. That ain't what Oi call fair weeding. Oi had it in my mind to do that bit of shrubbery the very morning Oi varlled down. If Oi had, Oi shouldn't ha' minded, not near so much. Now when Oi lies awake at night, Oi see those weeds—ramping.'

'She wor always a stirring ooman, sir,' explained her husband, 'an' it'll take her a bit to get used to having others stirring vur her. That's what Oi come to long ago, as Oi tell her. But telling ain't much use. Even the women have got to voind things out for themselves before they believe you.'

'You're a bit of a philosopher, I see, Potter.'

'Yes, sir,' interrupted his wife. 'Oi often tell him he'll shock the gentlefolk by his wild talk.'

'What does Miss—Joan say to it?' asked Lancaster, with a tender lingering on the name, and a consciousness of the foolishness which impelled him to drag it in on all subjects.

'Miss Joan don't know much about philosophy,' said Thomas, with a dry laugh. 'Oi've laid here so long that she thinks 'twas

what God Almighty made me vur, just as He
made the likes o' she to jump about and please
themselves.   That's her view of it, and nat'ral
enough—nat'ral enough.'

'No,' said Lancaster; 'you mustn't think
that.   She was very much distressed to hear
about Martha.'

'Ay, she's been used to seeing Martha
about,' said the old man.   ''Tis like the first
speck on a saucepan; it gets noticed and
cleaned off; but bymeby, when the bottom's
black, nobody takes no notice.'

'Oi'm sure Oi've allays kep' my saucepans
bright,' mourned Martha; 'and if Rose
Turner lets 'em all go to rack and ruin, Oi
can't help of it.   Then, maybe, you'll know,
Thomas, who it is as worked and worrited.
An' Oi do say as it's hard for me.'

'But about Miss Joan—don't you want to
hear how she gets on in London, and how
she looks?   Why, what a beautiful young
lady she is!'

' Her's comely, but her'll niver be half the woman my lady is. Oi've yeard as she's been to see the Queen. Oi reckon she won't be in no hurry to get back here, now she's up in the midst of all they vine folks.'

' Oh, she doesn't forget you. I think her heart's down here.'

Thomas gave his short laugh.

' Those young things don't know where their hearts is—don't know as they've got any till they begins to ache.'

' There now, Thomas, that's just like your talk. The gentleman will think as you're wishing Miss Joan a heartache.'

' No, no,' Lancaster answered. ' I don't believe anyone could wish that. And, you see, if she had not remembered you, I should not have been here. I came down on purpose to find out if you had all you wanted. To-morrow, as I said, I shall see her, and I can give her any message you care to send.' He added, putting something into Thomas's hand,

'This will help you to get any little thing you may need.'

The old man's thin fingers closed over the sovereign with an eagerness which Lancaster found unexpected.

'Thank ye, sir—thank ye kindly.' Perhaps he read something in the other's face, for he added : 'You medn't think now what makes me so pleased with your present? Well, Oi'll tell ye. All my presents come through Martha. It makes me feel more of a man' to have the money myself fust-hand, as you may say. Oh, Oi ain't gwine to keep it—it ain't that, an' it ain't like working for it; but if ever you was tied by the leg like me, you'd know the sort of veeling. Thank ye, sir. An' maybe you'll tell Miss Joan as Martha is toler'ble bad, but Oi'm a-seeing to her.'

Lancaster left the old woman lamenting her fate, and the old man chuckling over the reversal of things. On the whole, the visit

might be counted a failure for all he had
learnt of Joan, but it had added something
to his experience of human nature, a store on
which he set some value. Thomas evidently
found consolation in once more finding him
self on the same level with his wife.

'Joan said that he was the grumbler,' reflected the young man; 'but, good God!
what it must be to be laid aside like that—to
feel all the strength gone out of one—to be
dependent for everything—everything!'

He stopped and looked about him, drawing
a deep breath and noticing the broad shadow
which moved along by his side. The whole
country-side seemed full of life and strength;
a brisk breeze was blowing; a great waggon,
drawn by two powerful horses, rattled down
the hill; a couple of dogs, which might have
been Jack and Jill, were barking somewhere,
and children were shouting outside a small
school-house.

'I never thought about it so much before,'

Lancaster went on. ' I suppose I took it much as Joan takes it, and imagined people got used to maimed lives. That old fellow has never got used to his, and his wife's helplessness makes a sort of salve for his own. Queer, but not unnatural, when one comes to think of it.'

He walked briskly back to the station, his thoughts tenderly occupied with Joan. He saw her everywhere, the free, open, healthy country making just the setting which he fancied suited her best. How her face would brighten when she heard where he had been, and how many questions would be rained upon him! And now he would speak, now he would put it to the touch—not another week should pass without his making an opportunity to tell his tale. He would speak—it was the middle of June; well, by the beginning of August, or, at all events, the very moment Parliament rose, they might be married, and then they could get away abroad, or wherever she

would like to go. But, though he imagined
he left it to her, he really was forming very
distinct plans, for a man of his inexhaustible
energy would never rest content without
marking out the whither and the how; they
would go to Switzerland, and right across
Switzerland to the Engadine, coming back
by Nuremberg and some of the old German
towns. There was nothing out of the common
in such a programme, and he knew that
country so well that, had he been arranging
for the satisfaction of his own tastes, he
would have tried less beaten paths; but he
considered that all was new to Joan, and
that it would be well for her to see first the
places which must be known to her by name.

It cannot be said that he looked forward with
great pleasure to his connection with Lord
Medhurst. At the same time he did not dislike
the man, who was as conscientious as he was
narrow, and ruled his lines with careful regard
for what was just and right. He made mis-

takes in his treatment of his daughter, but his daughter was the most lovely, the most lovable of creatures, and if his system could produce such a result, it could not be far wrong. About Lady Medhurst he did not think at all. He had hardly noticed her. It was Joan—Joan who filled his fancies directly they got free from the yoke of hard work; Joan for whose sake he had wasted a day, and for whom he was going to face the weariness of a wedding to-morrow— smiling, however, when the thought flashed across him that he would keep an eye on the bridegroom, and see what a man should do who wanted to avoid looking like a fool.

At Roehampton there was some necessary preparation for this said wedding. It is true that Mrs. Gray always contrived to have a dress suitable for every occasion, and to look remarkably well in it, but Mary—Mary was too provoking!

She turned off each remonstrance with the

assurance that no one would look twice at her, and that her dress was not of the slightest consequence.

'But a wedding,' urged her mother—'at a wedding everyone makes some sort of an effort; you need not be quite so much of a brown mouse as usual. I don't know how it is, Mary, but you never seem to have anything to fall back upon. I do think it must be bad management.'

'You will do credit to the family, mother,' said Mary with a smile.

'But you make me feel very uncomfortable. People will suppose that I only think of myself, and I am sure it is just the contrary. I am quite as anxious that you should look well—more anxious, indeed,' she added with a smile which implied that this anxiety was caused by doubt. 'It is too late to do anything about a dress; if you must wear that old thing, you must : but a bonnet—I could run up to London and get you a bonnet, or you might telegraph to Basil—he has the best possible taste : he would not overdo it, if that is what you are afraid of.   Come, Mary !'

But Mary could not—would not.   She persisted that she should do very well, and that no one need fling her a second glance.

' I do think that it is very unkind of you, then,' said her mother, who had by no means given up the attack.   ' Unkind and obstinate.'

Mary was silent.   She did not even ask why ; she knew what was coming.

' It will vex Basil to see you looking a guy.   And it may be of consequence to him that his family should make a good impression.'

' I am very sorry if I am likely to stand in his way,' said Mary quietly.   ' Or—I don't know that I should be sorry.'

' Mary !'

For a moment Mary said nothing ; then she went on :

'He ought not to marry. He has no right to marry.'

'No right?'

'No. He cannot maintain his wife.'

'Then his wife may maintain him.'

'That is horrible—degrading!'

'Oh, my dear, certainly you ought to wear an antiquated dress to be in keeping with your ideas. Don't you read every day of young men marrying fortunes? Why should Basil set himself up on stilts above his age? Of one thing you may be sure. Anyone who marries him will have a charming husband.'

Apparently Mary was arguing without any hope of impressing her mother. She said suddenly, at this point:

'Does he expect to succeed?'

'He told me that it was a toss-up—twenty little things might affect it. That's why I want you to have a new bonnet for to-morrow.'

'Then I shall certainly not have a new bonnet,' returned Mary steadily.

'Only a bonnet! I have promised to say nothing about the dress. Come, let me write.'

Mrs. Gray pulled the writing things towards her. Mary turned pale.

'Mother, I cannot consent. Don't you understand? There is no money.'

'There must be some—somewhere,' said Mrs. Gray lightly.

'There is none. Basil has had it all.'

'Oh, well, my dear child, don't be tragic! I suppose it would not harm the woman to wait a little for her bill to be paid. They all know that you are to be trusted.'

'Yes; they know that,' said Mary bitterly. 'I am trusted because I refuse to run into debt.'

'Exactly. You *are* trusted; that is my point. Ah, General Murchison, how do you do? You're just in time to take my part, and do Mary a favour—a favour against her will.'

The gentleman thus addressed was a tall gaunt-looking man, with strongly-marked features and gray moustache. In spite of his long acquaintance, he shook hands with a little shyness and hesitation, looking from one to the other as if questioning. Mrs. Gray did not long keep him in doubt as to whom he belonged.

'Come and sit here,' she said, pointing to a seat near her sofa; 'you know your own particular chair by this time. Besides, Mary —Mary is too busy for conversation. She always is too busy, aren't you, Mary? She's always doing something—saving something; she has the cares of twice my years on her shoulders. She's so good!'

General Murchison tried to look at Miss Gray while her mother spoke in these laudatory terms, but the position of his chair prevented his seeing her, and he apparently lacked the courage to turn round and command a view. She did not, however, answer, and Mrs. Gray continued :

‘ All my preachings are opposed to the general aim of preachings. I want to make her less good, to implant a few seeds of vanity and frivolity. Do you know what I am trying for now ? A new bonnet. That ought not to be such a dreadful request, ought it ? I know I never wanted anyone to press it upon me. But you and I belong to a younger generation, and the world is ageing very fast when it is the mothers who have to stir their daughters into youth. It isn’t right —it puts them into a false position,’ she added, a little wistfully.

‘ Why is Miss Mary to have a new bonnet ?’ asked the General.

‘ For a wedding—a very gay wedding to-morrow.’

‘ Isn’t it too late ? I thought a bonnet was a serious matter.’

' Nothing can be too late when there is a telegraph and a London close to you,' said Mrs. Gray gaily. ' I want her to look her best. Can't you persuade her ?'

Upon this the General ventured to twist his long body so that at last he brought Mary within his range of view. She was working diligently, and did not glance up ; she looked very slight, very fragile.

' If I can do anything in the matter,' he began slowly, ' I hope you will command me. Can I take a telegram to the office ?'

' There, Mary. Now it is perfectly easy. You ought to do it, if only to please me.'

Mary was sitting with her back to the light, and it is possible that General Murchison did not see the hot colour which rushed up over her face. She said in a low voice, and trying to laugh :

' I am very sorry that my poor bonnet should be so unpopular ; but I must keep to it.'

Mrs. Gray made a gesture of annoyance.

'Well, it is very irritating.'

General Murchison seemed to consider slowly; then he said, quite simply, and without apparently intending a compliment :

'I have never seen you in anything that was not charming.'

'That is charming of *you*,' said Mrs. Gray, with a light laugh ; 'but I hoped you would have been a stronger ally. However, when once Mary has made up her mind, she is iron —adamant ; and I have given up attempting to persuade her, so it is as well that you should not attempt it.'

This time General Murchison appeared to be sensible of a little disturbance in the air, for he rose up, walked to the window, and changed the subject.

'Your garden is as gay as usual. You have an excellent show of roses.'

'But it is not like yours, a miracle of neat-ness. We rub along and make the best of our poor little collection of plants, which have had to struggle through the winter by the help of a lamp or a night-light—which is it, Mary, that you allow them ? Nobody knows what allowances ought to be made for us.'

'Because it is very far from anyone's thoughts to suppose that you require any,' he said stoutly. 'Everything here looks well-ordered and cheerful. If I have fewer weeds I have not half your flowers. Mrs. Gray, do you remember that you promised to be good enough to show me that old miniature of Walpole ?'

'So I did ! I will get it. No, thank you, Mary ; I couldn't explain where you would find it.'

She went away, and General Murchison came back and sat on the edge of a chair near Mary. He was silent for a moment, and then said suddenly :

'I am afraid that something has distressed you.'

Mary looked up timidly, but she said, with a frank smile :

'It is nothing—at least, it ought to be nothing. As you know, we are poor, and I am obliged to be careful, and mother has a very liberal soul and thinks me stingy——'

'You are not,' he interrupted.

'I don't know—I am not sure. Sometimes I feel very mean and petty, and as if I couldn't enlarge my ideas even if I ought. Happily it doesn't seem as if that would ever be my duty.'

There was rather a pained look on her listener's face, and he fidgeted on his chair.

'It appears to me that more falls upon your shoulders than should be there by rights.'

'Oh,' she said, 'it is necessary. Who is there but me ? My mother would do it if she could, but she can't ; she hasn't a frugal mind. That's what I have. And as I told you, sometimes I can't make out whether it is a vice or a virtue.' She coloured again slightly. 'I beg your pardon. I don't know what has made me say all this.'

'No,' he said more quickly, 'it is seldom enough that you will speak of yourself. You are always at work for others; it is what they think, what they feel, which is of consequence —one is never allowed so much as a peep at your own thoughts or wishes. I come here very often, and it is always the same story. You are holding up the burden of the house, you are standing aside in the shadow, and there is no one to see it; it appears to be a matter of course. I wish, I wish——'

His tone had become more impetuous, and as he said these last few words he had risen and stood looking down strangely at her. But what he wished remained unspoken, for at this moment Sissy dashed into the room, hugging a box in her arms.

'Aunt Mary! look, look what daddy has sent me! and I don't know what it is, but it's sure to be booful.'

Mrs. Gray was close behind, and General Murchison must see the box unpacked, and an expensive dancing dog taken out, and then he must look at the miniature. It seemed to Mary that she was living in a sort of dream— how much was real ? He went away at last, wishing her good-bye in his usual slow shy manner, and she heard Sissy's little treble chattering away to him in the garden, and then Mrs. Gray's laugh.

'Can I, can I ? Mary, you never help me ! But some day, you know, I shall have to make up my mind whether I will or whether I won't, and I ought to know beforehand. I am sure he has given me opportunities enough. What do you wish yourself ? It is a terrible thing to think of giving up one's independence, and then that odd shy manner of his—I shall never break him of it ; he will carry it to his grave. It always provokes me. But—but life would be easier, a little more butter for one's bread, an end to all this detestable scraping and pinching, which is making an old woman of you before your time. Oh, I do care, Mary, though you don't suppose it! I think of you when I think of the General. Come, there's time yet. If I make up my mind to say yes, will you telegraph for a bonnet? You won't? Well, then, if you are so obstinate, I'm by no means sure that I shall ever consent, for I don't see why I should be the one to make all the sacrifices.'

CHAPTER XV.

CONSTANCE had been married. Constance, after protesting that she could not understand why people should be so foolish as to cry at their own weddings, had broken down so ignominiously that Susan, who was considered the bridesmaid-in-charge, went through a time of great anxiety, and it was always declared afterwards by her other sisters that a choked sob was the only response Constance ever made to the questions which she had declared she should answer so bravely.

'Nothing more than a gasp, Arthur,' said Elizabeth in a commiserating tone. 'And I

am sure that a gasp has no meaning. If I
were you, I should insist upon having it all
over again. She has made no promises. If
ever I am asked I shall be obliged to say that
I heard not a word.'

'Oh, Elizabeth! how can you?' said poor
Constance, who had not quite recovered
herself. 'I am sure it did very well,
and Uncle Hugh has not said anything
about it.'

'Luckily, he is a friend of the Bishop's, so
he may be able to set things right; but I
shouldn't be quite comfortable if I were
Arthur—I shouldn't, indeed. Mamma, here
is poor Arthur wanting a little assurance.
You have known Constance a good long
while; do you think she was wilfully silent
to-day?'

'Arthur does not want any assurance,' said
Mrs. Ashton, tenderly kissing her newly-
married daughter. 'He would not have
wished for anything different. It was natural

enough that she should be a little upset, wasn't it, Arthur? We should all have felt a little hurt, I think, if she could have gone away from us without a tear. But it went off beautifully.'

'There, you have had your comfort; and in order that mamma may stay and admire you for a few minutes, I will go and talk to other people,' said Elizabeth, moving off. The next moment she touched Lady Millicent. 'I have seen nothing, and shall see nothing, of you in all this hubbub—perhaps a little later?'

'You look tired already.'

'It's only the dress. Imagine me in reseda! But, after deducting Susan and me, you five others look very creditable.'

'Joan Medhurst looks more than creditable. She is lovely.'

'I suppose she is. I wish she had never come to town.'

'Why?' said Lady Millicent quietly.

' Because she is turning heads that should have been wiser.'

' You mean Sir Henry Lancaster's ? That is more than a turning of heads. I am sure it is quite serious with him, from what I have noticed to-day, and I hope it is with her.'

Elizabeth looked at her wistfully.

' Ah, Millicent,' she said, ' you are a hundred times better than I ! But I can't stay; I perceive a neglected Maxwell, and must march her round the presents. Have you seen the table of mustard-pots ? Constance and Arthur were quite serious about it; they saw nothing comic in the idea, bless them !'

Sir Henry Lancaster was there, as will have been gathered. He had even gone to the church, where nobody expected him, and where he arrived late, but contrived to get near a pillar from which he commanded a view of Joan. He had eyes for no one else. She was looking singularly pretty, the soft fresh colouring of her dress setting off her young beauty, and her eyes full of eager interest. Her lover's heart went out to her. He felt a strong yearning to claim her, to hold her fast, and, for the first time, a jealousy of the other men who were near. When the carriages reached Albion Street, he could hardly go through the necessary courtesies before making his way to Joan, and one or two persons, by whom he had pushed unceremoniously, were confirmed in their opinion that Sir Henry Lancaster was a bear.

'At last!' he said, standing before her.

'At last?' repeated Joan, smiling. 'Why, you have only just come, haven't you?'

'Only just? It has seemed ages to me until I reached you.'

She looked down and blushed, smiling. Something in his voice had made her heart beat a little more quickly. He held out towards her a white pink.

'Guess where this comes from.'

'That? How can I? I don't know. Is it anything particular? Do tell me!'

He was silent for a few moments, enjoying her perplexity; then he bent down.

'It is from old Martha's garden.'

'From Martha's garden! From Ashbury! You have been there to see her? Oh, how is she? How good of you—how very good of you!'

'I went yesterday. I could not bear that you should be longing for news and not have it. I went down, and I saw Ashbury, and I saw Martha and old Thomas.'

'And is she better?—really better? Does Mrs. Jones behave properly?'

'Beef-tea seemed to be coming in steadily. That's the great thing, isn't it? And old Thomas bade me tell you he was looking after his wife.'

'Old Thomas! I dare say! When she has to get everything for him.'

'I suspect he enjoys feeling himself on the

same level once more.   He was quite cheerful—not a bit grumbly.'

'Then I think it is horrid of him,' said the
young girl indignantly.   'Poor dear old
Martha! But I am very glad about the beef-
tea.   Mrs. Jones isn't a bad old thing, only
she has favourites.   Did you see her?'

'No.   But I saw your garden'—he
dropped his voice—'and I fancied at every
turn that you stood before me.   You don't
know how much I care for Ashbury.'

Joan laughed a little uneasily.

'It seemed to me,' he went on, 'that I
knew it all before I came to it.   Do you
remember that night—that first night that I
ever saw you?   Well, then you told me about
your home, and I have not forgotten one
word.   I have gone over each picture again
and again.   Did you know, I wonder, what
you were doing?—how your innocent words
were writing themselves on my heart?'

Something in his look, his tone, some only

half-repressed thrill of passion, frightened her. She gave him a quick glance, and was turning away, when he detained her.

'Joan,' he said in a strong low voice, 'do you know? Do you know that from that moment I have loved you with all the strength of my heart, and set myself to win you? My darling, will you come to me?—will you trust me?'

He was interrupted. They had been standing by the window. Joan was partly hidden by a curtain, and Lancaster stood so that his broad shoulders shut out all that would otherwise have been visible. People had crowded to see the presents at the other end of the room, and the two had been to all intents and purposes alone. It was this which had led him on until he had forgotten everything but the intense longing which forced his words from him, and seemed to compel her to listen. But the world was not to be so thrust out. It had surged back again, filled the vacant space, and now Mrs.

Russell found herself so awkwardly close that, although she had a moment's amazed awakening, she was obliged to speak to Joan.

'And I never felt so uncomfortable in my life,' she confided afterwards to her husband. 'Sir Henry gave me a look which he meant. But who would have supposed it possible! I thought it odd, I confess, that day at the House; and I presume he is a young man still, and has been caught by a pretty face, but—I never expected it to come to this! I don't believe she's in the least the wife for him.'

'What about your Basil Gray scare?'

'Of course that was absurd, except as a flirtation. But I will say that he's a dangerously pleasant fellow, and a good deal more attractive to a young girl than Sir Henry. Sir Henry's a man a woman must either be very much in love with or dislike. I can't fancy his laying himself out to be

agreeable. Oh dear, I wish I had not been
forced into that corner! I do hate being
thought a marplot.'

' Lancaster's not the man to mind a small
obstacle,' said her husband, by way of consolation. ' But I believe it's all your fertile
fancy. At any rate, Gray looked as right as
a trivet. What a fellow he is! You'd really
suppose he'd ten thousand a year. And how
comes he to have such a quiet body for a
sister?'

' Isn't she a frump! But it's rather a
sweet little face for all that.'

Major Russell was right in supposing that
a small difficulty in the way was not likely to
affect Lancaster beyond a momentary vexa-
tion. He had said his say, and he meant to
force an opportunity, if force were needed, to
get his answer. All that he had seen of
Joan was a startled face, for, although she
had thought of him as a lover, she had not
expected such a sudden onslaught, and his

words had been spoken with an energy
which seemed as if it would sweep her—
breathless—away. She had not disliked this
impetuosity, yet, oddly enough, it made her
shrink from her own resolve as she had not
shrunk before, and she felt as if she could
not answer him as he wished — she no
longer felt as if she knew what she wished
herself.

Lancaster had drawn sharply back when
Mrs. Russell offered her inopportune greet-
ings, and stood stolidly waiting for his lost
moment to come again. It cost him something to be patient, more especially as he
was at no time remarkable for the grace;
but circumstances often force it upon us, and
here circumstances were made up of one
person after another—finally, and most per-
sistently, Mrs. Gray.

'I have been looking for you, Henry,
and I find you just where I hoped. Will
you introduce me to Miss Medhurst?'

Joan, who still felt slightly bewildered or overwhelmed—she would not have known which—was really grateful for the interruption, and as—here also without knowing why—anyone connected with Basil Gray interested her, she looked at his mother with her most charming smile. She was immediately attracted by her, or by the admiration she read in her eyes. Though she had long left youth behind her, Mrs. Gray had managed to preserve its qualities, and preferred young people to her own contemporaries. No one could have a keener appreciation of beauty and brightness.

'I am very glad to have met you at last,' she said. 'I have heard so much about you from my boy.'

'I know Mr. Gray,' murmured Joan.

'Have you seen him to-day? I always pity a young man at this sort of gathering, when it is almost impossible to speak to the persons one would choose, and often

enough one gets driven up against the very
people one has been doing one's best to
avoid. The young feel that to be so in-
sufferable; it is only we older ones—such as
my nephew and myself,' she added, looking
at Lancaster with a laugh—'who have
learnt endurance.'

The girl glanced at Sir Henry; he was
standing square and unsmiling. But Mrs.
Gray meant to be answered.

'Don't you agree with me, Henry?'

'I beg your pardon, I did not follow
you.'

'Well, we'll put it that you belong to an
older generation than Basil.'

'Oh, I don't pretend to compete with
Basil,' he said grimly.

At this moment Nan hurried up.

'Here is the missing bridesmaid!' she
cried. 'Come, Joan, we are waiting for
you; your father seems to believe you have
run away. We are all to go down with

Constance, and form a touching group at the end of the table. The poor things have hardly time for their tea.'

Joan went willingly. She was not prepared with an answer to the question which still rang in her ears, and she was glad to escape. Perhaps, away from his strong feelings, which found vent in word and look, and seemed to demand so much, she might get back her decision. She thought she would. But for the present, strangely enough, she wanted to escape.

Constance was almost herself again. Congratulations on her lot, and admiration of her presents, had restored her, and she was thoroughly enjoying her position.

'It really is very nice,' she confided to Lady Millicent. 'Of course the church and all that part is upsetting, just for the moment, but Arthur was as kind as possible about it, and declared he didn't mind. I was so afraid he might. But that is such a comfort with Arthur : there is no putting him out. He vows he was in a blue fright himself.'

'Oh, you both behaved very well,' said Millicent ; 'and I am sure everything has gone quite smoothly.'

'I hope my veil won't come off; Susie says it can't,' went on Constance. 'I like your dresses so much, and so does Arthur, though he did wish for blue. But I am quite proud of my bridesmaids. I shall long to see the photograph. Nan, mind I have the photograph directly, or perhaps I had better tell Susie, to make sure. Dear old Susie! she never forgets anything.' A tear fell, and Constance hastily turned away her head, but the next moment recovered herself. 'And you see, Nan, you need not have been unhappy about the bridesmaids' presents ; you may always depend on Arthur's taste. I am so glad you all like them so much. I must say I think the black pearl for the ball in the centre of the dear little gold racket a splendid idea.'

She was very happy, and no one could find fault with her innocent exaltation in her Arthur, though to others he might appear a commonplace hero. Presently Colonel Ashton came to tell his daughter that it was time for her to change her dress. Susan hurried away with her, and the other bridesmaids, released from duty, were scattered about the room, Joan carefully avoiding Lancaster.

He bided his time quietly, having every intention of securing it somehow, and therefore being able to afford to wait. But his eyes followed her every movement, and his face darkened when he saw that Basil Gray was by her side. Basil, indeed, presented no signs of the rejected lover, and Joan was rather piqued to find him as amusingly light-hearted as before. At the same time it was a relief not to have lost him as a

companion or a partner, for she had feared
that there would be no more enchanting
dancing, and was ready to cry at the thought.
He stayed by her, amused her by his comments upon the people, told her stories, and
succeeded in making her wish with a sigh
that he were only Lancaster. When—at
intervals—her thoughts reverted to that
decision which lay before her, she felt her
resolution yet more shaken, and scarcely
believed that she could make up her mind
to accept Sir Henry.

But—but it was Lord Medhurst who gave
a fillip to her wavering resolution. He caught
her just as she and Gray were laughing merrily
at some jest of Basil's, and something in his
eye made Joan's heart sink into the depths.

' Let me have a word with you, my dear,'
was what he said.

' Yes, papa,' said she, moving aside reluctantly.

' I must request that you do not conceal

yourself behind curtains or in corners, as was the case just now. Your cousins were looking for you everywhere, and appealed to your mother and to me, but neither of us could assist them. I can assure you we found it very unpleasant to be unable to say where you were.'

' I was in the room all the while. I was not hiding myself,' said Joan.

' But you allowed yourself to be hidden. I do not desire to remark any more about it, only do not let it happen again ; and let me ask you to keep near me or your mother for the remainder of the time.'

Rebellion, active rebellion, rose in her heart. How was it possible to endure this constant check ? She could not, she would not. Anything was better. It seemed to her that more than one person watched the lecture with a smile, and the blood rushed into her face. Hardly knowing what she did, she flung Lancaster an imploring look.

He was at that moment — Joan being separated from him—talking to Lady Millicent, whom he had not seen since her return from Denningham.

'You have not been long in the country,' he said, 'but long enough to be all the better for wholesome air and exercise. Happy person !'

'Do you love the real country so much, or is it only a country which it pleases you to imagine that attracts you ?'

'I mean downright country. Pigs, poultry, all that sort of thing—no neighbours, and no politics.'

She shook her head.

'Have you ever tried it ?'

'I tried it yesterday.'

'Where ?'

'At Ashbury.   I ran down to Ashbury.'

She was silent for an instant, looking down. Then she lifted her face, and said hesitatingly, but with smiling lips :

' Perhaps that was an enchanted country ?'

He was not displeased.

' Perhaps.'

' And you are under the spell.'

' Who would not be ?'

' No,' she repeated faintly—'who would not be ? But, remember, you have to live your life, and, whether you believe it or not, that life belongs to the world of men. Anywhere else you would be miserable and remorseful, because you have no right to let the work given to you drop out of your hands.'

He stood silent.

' Is it worth much, after all ?'

' It is worth your life to you,' she said earnestly. ' How often you have talked of what there is to be done, how many wrongs there are to be fought, how many abuses put down, how, if a man cares for his duty, he cannot turn aside into more pleasant paths ! No; the country would not be a right or

happy place for you.   You must keep your
harness on.'

He glanced at her.

'Yes,' he said, 'you are right—quite right.
I don't mean to give up work, even——' It
was just then that Joan cast her imploring
look at him, and his words died away abruptly.
'I beg your pardon,' he said quickly to Millicent; 'I believe I am wanted.'

She watched him wistfully — saw him
shoulder his way to Joan's side, and look
at her with a smile which softened all the
rugged lines of his face.   Colonel Ashton
came up at this moment.

'I hope your father isn't bored,' he said
uneasily.   'They'll soon be off.   It'll seem
strange without Con, won't it?   But, there,
Arthur's a good fellow, a very good fellow,
and she's every chance of happiness, I do
believe.   It would be selfish of us to want to
keep the young ones in the nest.'

'Ah, well, I can't spare Millicent,' said

Lord Waterton, who had just come up. 'All very well for you, Ashton, with two or three others left to you, but if Millicent takes herself off, what on earth am I to do? I give you fair warning, Mil, that I shan't stand it quietly.'

She answered him gaily that there was no fear; it would be a long time before anyone wanted her so badly as he did.

'All the better,' returned her father in the same tone; but she saw his eyes resting with dissatisfaction upon Sir Henry and Joan, and it was a relief to her when Elizabeth Ashton came through the throng.

'Where is Eva Maxwell? Oh, I see her! Millicent, all the bridesmaids are to be in the passage; will you please go out? Constance will be down in a minute.'

When Lancaster reached Joan's side, he could not say a word to her, but she looked at him and smiled, and look and smile made the strong man's heart throb. In the little

movement which followed he managed to
whisper 'I must speak to you,' and she
whispered back, 'Upstairs—afterwards.'

Poor Constance! It was hard that the
tears at which she had jeered should get the
upper hand with such persistency that they
almost drowned her farewells. She clung
first to one and then the other, and if Arthur
had not displayed quite an unexpected spirit
in support of her father's assurance that they
would miss the train at Victoria, there is no
knowing how she would have been got away.
But it was over at last, the carriage had
driven off, and the rest of the world were pre-
paring to depart. Joan passed the dining-
room door and her father's back with a
delicious sensation of revolt, and ran lightly
upstairs. At the head stood Lancaster.

'There are people in the drawing-room,'
he said; 'come in here'—drawing her into
a small den at the back. 'Now!'

There was triumph, exaltation in his tone—

he had grasped her arms above the wrists, and stood looking down upon her with a dominating gaze which she felt without seeing. But as she was silent his voice changed to passionate pleading.

'Joan—my darling,' he said, ' say one word: can you love me ? Will you marry me ?'

He did not get his word, but he got another answer. The girl lifted her head, threw it back and smiled at him. She had made up her mind, there was no shrinking, and the next moment he had clasped her in his arms.

CHAPTER XVI.

'Joan—have you seen Joan?'

'Isn't she to be found? She was here just now. Nan, is Joan in the drawing-room?'

'I didn't see her.'

'It is vexatious of the child,' said Lady Medhurst in a low voice, 'because her father desired her to keep near us, and she ought to attend to his wishes.'

'People get swept away in spite of the best intentions in such a crowd as this,' said Mrs. Ashton good-naturedly. 'I am afraid my daughters are generally left to take care of themselves. She can't be very far away—however, shall I tell Susie to look for her?'

Susie was found and despatched, while Lord Medhurst peered about, greatly discomposed by the fact that six other young ladies were clad in the same colour as his daughter, and yet more that after his injunction Joan had taken herself out of reach. It was an act of independence such as he could hardly brook.

Down came the messenger again with no tidings. Joan was not in the drawing-room.

'She must be ill,' said Lady Medhurst, making her way to the staircase, and almost hoping that here lay the explanation for such strange conduct. But when she looked into the drawing-room, there was the truant, talking unconcernedly to three or four others, one of them Sir Henry Lancaster. Lady Medhurst had more tact than her husband; she only said smilingly :

'Ah, here you are, Joan ! We were wondering where you had hidden yourself, and your father is anxious to go.'

No more quakings, no terror. Down the stairs, behind her mother, marched Joan, cool and indifferent, and behind Joan was Sir Henry. At the foot he touched her arm.

' Do you really wish me not to come in now ?' he asked in a low voice.

' Not now ; oh no, don't come now ; come later—come to dinner. Don't let them see anything now !' in an answering whisper.

He lifted his broad shoulders, but she must of course have her own way, and there was a dancing light in her eyes which would alone have been irresistible. So at Lady Medhurst's desire he extracted Lord Medhurst, who was just—for the third time—on the point of addressing a sister of the bridegroom, under the idea that he had captured Joan, and saw his love depart in safe keeping.

Joan's heart was beating, but this time it was with eager delight. By one word she could alter the whole position of affairs. Instead of the displeasure which was pre-

sently to descend upon her head, instead of
the lecturings, the fault-findings to which, in
the natural order of things, she was doomed
to listen—instead of these, one little sentence
breathed by her, and—hey, presto! all would
be changed. No longer a schoolgirl to be
scolded, she would be a person of importance,
for whom, as the chosen of the distinguished
Sir Henry, she was fondly assured that her
father would feel almost respect. And the
delight of this conviction was so great, and
so much overpassed any other feeling connected with her engagement, that she even
looked forward to the summons which had
never before failed to send her heart down,
down to its lowest depths.

This time it was more severe, more
judicial. Before it had been, 'My dear, I
should be glad to speak to you for a moment
before going upstairs;' now it was, 'Joan, I
must request you to come into my room.'
Lady Medhurst hesitated, but her daughter

flung her a petition through her eyes, which
she interpreted as a desire to have someone
to put in a word for her, whereas really Joan
only wanted her triumph to be complete.
Lord Medhurst sat down, crossed his legs,
and motioned his daughter towards a chair.

'I must own,' he began in a tone of displeasure, 'that I have been both surprised
and annoyed this afternoon.   It appears to
me, Joan, that I expressed myself quite clearly
to the effect that you were to remain near
your mother and myself, instead of which, for
the second time, you contrived to conceal
yourself, and to require that a very un-
seemly and unnecessary search should be
made.'

Lord Medhurst paused.   Generally, Joan
would have been by this time reduced to con-
fusion, but to-day, though he could hardly
credit it, there were signs, unmistakable signs,
of callous indifference.   She looked at him
instead of on the ground, and, if such a thing

were possible, a smile trembled on her lips.
He became more impressive.

'It can hardly, I conceive, be necessary for
me to point out to you that such inattention
to my wishes is both unbecoming and dis-
respectful. The only excuse that presents
itself to me is the possibility of your not
having understood. I always endeavour to
express myself with clearness, but you were
perhaps not giving me your whole attention?'

'There was a good deal of talking, and the
child might have been a little bewildered,' put
in Lady Medhurst. 'Was that it? Did you
understand your father?'

'Yes; I knew he wanted me to stay near,
but I couldn't,' returned Joan boldly.

'Couldn't—could not. Do not clip your
words,' said her father irritably. 'I confess I
hardly understand. You could not?'

'You treat me like a child—I am not a
child, I am grown up!' cried she with excitement. 'Other girls are not told to stay close

by their fathers and mothers—it makes me ridiculous. Someone had something to say to me, and you would have liked me to come and say, " Please, papa, may I go and speak to so and so ?" I wouldn't do it. I went. And I was quite right.'

If a thunderbolt had fallen at Lord Medhurst's feet he would scarcely have been more discomposed. This from Joan—this from the well-trained daughter—this the result of his system! He stared at her blankly ; he could hardly find breath to exclaim :

' Joan !'

' It is true, papa,' she cried, jumping up ; ' and if you bring me to London and let me go about in the world, you ought not to behave as if I were a little girl and could not be trusted. It isn't fair !'

' Hush, Joan !' said her mother softly. ' Who wanted to speak to you ?'

' Sir Henry Lancaster.'

Here was the first heavy gun brought up

and discharged. Hitherto it had been only light musketry, fired, if the truth must be told, with quite as much amazement as it had been received ; but this—this was a different matter. It produced all the effect she expected. Lord Medhurst put on his double eye-glasses and looked at her, and Lady Medhurst could not repress a movement of satisfaction.

'Do you mind,' she said very gently, 'letting us know what he had to say ?'

'Do you mind ?' Here was a change already. Up came Joan's great reserve.

'He asked me to marry him.'

A pause. Lord Medhurst looked at his wife, who was visibly startled.

'My dear Joan !' she cried the next moment.

Lord Medhurst took off his glasses, uncrossed his legs, and leaned forward, as she got up and kissed her daughter.

'My dear,' he said, 'I am bound to admit

that you have given me a very reasonable excuse for your conduct.   Am I to understand that you are prepared to accept Sir Henry?'

'I told him I would.'

'After consultation with us,' her father corrected quickly.   'Well, my dear, I am glad to assure you that such a marriage has my warmest approval.   Sir Henry Lancaster is both an excellent and a distinguished man. It is really an honour to you that your first proposal should have come from such a quarter.'

'Oh, not my first,' Joan remarked carelessly.   'They're always doing it.'

Lord Medhurst's face at this speech was a study.   Blank amazement mingled with disapprobation, while gratified pride at Lancaster's offer overpowered both.

'Well, well,' he said hastily; 'I should have supposed—however, we will not speak of that.   It is enough that your mother and I—for I am sure I express her sentiments with my own—are thoroughly gratified with your choice. I presume that Sir Henry will take an early opportunity of ascertaining that he has our sanction? Indeed, I almost wonder he did not come back with us.'

' He wanted to, but I told him not,' said the young girl.

Wanted to! Told him not! Poor Lord Medhurst gasped over the grammar and the audacity, but he only gasped. Already Joan stood on a different level, and if presently the habit of correction would prove too strong for him, for the first minutes he had the tact to hold it back. After her kiss Lady Medhurst had sat down again, but she still held her child's hand, and she gave it a pressure as she said:

' Sir Henry Lancaster is all we could wish for you, my dearest Joan, so long as you are sure of your own heart. But do not hurry— do not accept him without reflection. His offer must have taken you by surprise——'

The girl opened her eyes.

'Oh no, mamma!'

'Do you mean that you—you had any expectation of such a step on his part?'

'Oh yes, of course. I was sure it would come.'

Lord Medhurst hesitated; then:

'Would it not have been well, my dear, to have mentioned your suspicions to your mother? I am not blaming you, understand; only that appears to me as if it would have been the more natural course.'

To this Joan made no answer. When the first burst of unaccustomed vehemence was over, it was not easy for her to repeat her complaints of her father, for she was by nature timid. It was enough to have turned the threatened lecture into a triumph, and to feel the amazement with which they looked at her, which indeed caused her intense delight.

'Is Sir Henry going to write?' inquired Lady Medhurst.

'He is coming to dinner,' the young girl rejoined.

'Did you ask him?'

'Certainly. Wasn't it right?'

'Oh, quite right,' her mother hastened to reply. She hardly knew what to say next. 'Will you not go upstairs, then, and rest for a little while?'

'I am not tired,' said Joan, smiling. 'But I may as well go upstairs, unless you are going out again.'

As the door closed behind her, Lady Medhurst got up and took a chair close to her husband. She looked moved, and it almost seemed as if there were tears in her eyes.

'Oh, Walter!' she exclaimed, 'I hope—I trust the child knows what she is doing! She takes it with as much ease as if to engage one's self in marriage were an everyday occurrence. I assure you, I looked at her with amazement. Do you think she knows?'

'She is very young,' said her husband, re-

turning to his formula, 'and I own that some
of her expressions this afternoon gave me a
disagreeable shock. But she was probably
more excited than you suppose, and in whose
hands could she be so well placed as in Sir
Henry's ? Naturally, much remains for her
to learn. We have done what we could, and
I had looked forward to a longer time of in-
direct instruction. Indeed, I am surprised
that a man of Lancaster's powers should be
content with a girl whose character is as yet
so immature. But he possibly desires to
mould her while she is young and tractable,
and I cannot but feel that his wish to make
her his wife affords me the liveliest satisfaction.'

'Yes,' agreed Lady Medhurst—'yes, certainly. But does she love him ?'

'My dear Emily, she esteems him, which is
better. Heaven knows,' he went on with
feeling, 'that it is not his position nor his
talents which I chiefly regard in this matter.

He is a man of sterling worth, respected alike
by friend and foe, and it is for this reason that
I especially rejoice Joan should have found so
good a husband.'

'And so do I—indeed I do! The only
drawback I feel is that it should have been
so hastily decided. I fear whether she knows
her own mind.'

'She spoke of others,' said Lord Medhurst,
with hesitation.

His wife sighed.

'It amazed me. We have thought of her
as a child. Who can they be? And it is so
strange that she should not have given us her
confidence!'

'I must have pointed out that reserve as a
very serious error,' said Lord Medhurst, 'if
it had not been for this event. As it is, I
imagine it had better be passed over. Lancaster will for the future, let us hope'—he
also sighed—'share her thoughts, and the
parents must be content to stand aside and

watch her development under what are doubt-
less unexpected circumstances. I had trusted
that two or three years' watchfulness and
careful training would have produced an excellent effect, and I am still not without hope
that in Lancaster's hands the same results
may be reached. She is exceedingly docile,
and will no doubt follow his lead, and adapt
herself to whatever life he considers de-
sirable.'

Was this so? Lady Medhurst would not
for worlds have contradicted her husband, for
whose judgment she had the greatest respect.
Yet her mother's heart told her a different
tale, and Joan's outburst that day confirmed
her fears. It appeared that she could keep
her own counsel : was she also keeping back
an undergrowth of longings, ambitions, self-
seekings, which she fancied this marriage was
to gratify? Thinking of Sir Henry Lancaster,
she could conceive that he was a man whom
a woman might love with all her heart, but

whom, not loving, she might grow to hate. Nothing in the girl's manner had given her the idea of much love. She was forced, however, to own that she was not in touch with her daughter, and that Joan had proved that she could keep a good deal to herself.

Joan had not half her mother's doubts as she dressed for dinner. She was, indeed, in the full flush of triumphant delight, and she reflected with great glee upon the lecture which she had so successfully parried.

' Papa had so much to say ; he was brimming over with rebuke. I could see him bringing out all my wickednesses one by one, like poor little prisoners dragged up for sentence. What would have been bad enough for their punishment, I wonder ? I should have stood there hanging my head, and feeling as I used to feel when I didn't know my lessons, only worse—oh yes, this would have been much worse—and then down it would have come ! What would it have been ? Let

me see. Oh, I know! I shouldn't have been
allowed to go to Lady Avonshire's ball to-
morrow night — that would have been one thing
certain. Papa has been trying to slip out of
it all this week, and he would have jumped
at an excuse. Only imagine! To have lost
such a ball! Why, it's worth marrying Sir
Henry only to make sure of that. They can't
treat me now as if I were a little girl with all
my hair down my back. I shall be somebody
of consequence, and shall be allowed to put
in *my* oar, and to say what I like and what
I don't like. Not another lecture do I go to,
that's one thing! I'm sure girls don't go to
lectures when they're engaged ; at any rate, I
shall make Sir Henry say that I am not to.
He's very nice and big, and able to stand up for
one, and he's very much in love, so that I
shall only have just to give him a hint. It *is*
a pity he can't dance, but he can't.' She
paused blankly. 'Oh no, he can't for a
minute suppose that I should give it up

because I'm engaged, or married, or anything. Absurd! Of course he can't. Give
up dancing at nineteen! No, thank you. I
should break it all off if he had any such idea.
I might just as well be Joan Medhurst and go
to lectures. With Basil Gray there could
have been no doubt. Poor Basil! how nice
he was to-day! But, then, other things would
not have been at all comfortable, and—oh
dear, imagine papa's horror! Besides, I
needn't be afraid. I can make Sir Henry do
anything. I'll make him say I *must* go to
balls. Papa will listen to him. Papa respects
him awfully—it was such fun seeing his face
just now, when I told him that he made me
ridiculous!'

There was a knock.

'May I come in?' asked Lady Medhurst.
'Ah! I see that you are ready. Maria said
that you had sent her away, and I dare say
you liked best to be alone. But, my dear, I
felt that I must come and tell you how pleased

your father and I are with your choice. I don't think anyone'—kissing her—'could have been more to your father's liking. Only —perhaps I feel more than he does a fear whether you have not allowed yourself to be too hurried. You are very young and inexperienced, you know, and such an offer as this is one which might well bewilder a young girl who has heard Sir Henry spoken of as a distinguished man, likely to rise to still higher honours, and who might allow herself to be a little dazzled at being singled out by his admiration and love. My dear,' she ended earnestly, ' that is most natural, but it is not enough.'

' I don't think I am dazzled,' said Joan, smiling.

The mother looked at her and sighed.

' You spoke of others. Do you mean that you have received other proposals ?'

' Oh yes,' said the young girl, still smiling. ' The last was Lord Islington.'

'And you thought so little of it that you did not even mention it!'

'I suppose such things are common enough, unless one is——'

'What?'

'Ugly,' returned Joan, with dancing eyes.

Lady Medhurst felt dumbfounded, afraid to pursue her questions. It did not seem as if Joan were inexperienced at all. It was she who felt simple and shy by her side.

'Then,' she said slowly, 'you really love Sir Henry?'

'I like him well enough.'

The mother opened her mouth to exclaim, and closed it again.

'I don't think I understand you, Joan,' she said at last, with a sigh. 'In my day we were more disturbed by the thought of such a thing as has come to you to-day.'

'Do you wish to see me disturbed, mamma?'

'I should like to feel that it was a serious matter to you, not hastily entered upon.'

'Oh, I haven't been hasty. Isn't papa satisfied?'

'Oh, perfectly, perfectly!' Lady Medhurst said hurriedly. 'Dear Joan, understand that nothing could please us better; it was only for yourself that I was anxious, from the fear that you might not really know your own heart. But you seem to have thought it out, and so——' She broke off abruptly. 'Are you quite ready? I think I hear Sir Henry's voice.' Another time she might have added, 'You look very nice,' but now it hardly seemed as if Joan would be satisfied with so limited a tribute; apparently she expected something more brilliant.

Joan liked her evening very well. Lancaster's admiring looks did not confuse her at all. After dinner they two went out on the little balcony, over which the striped awning was still stretched. Lancaster dragged

out a couple of chairs, and the two sat there
in the soft sweet dusk, with the scent of
mignonette about them, and the stars twink-
ling out of the sky. It was all very quiet
and peaceful. Lancaster drew a long breath
and stretched himself back in his chair.

'Joan,' he demanded, 'when are we to be
married ?'

'I don't know.'

'You don't mean to keep me on tenter-
hooks as some poor wretched men are kept ?
I give you fair warning I am not patient
enough for that treatment.'

She looked at him and laughed.

'Oh, you must learn to be patient.'

'Well, I shall choose my own course of
instruction, and it shall have nothing to do
with the wedding-day. Lord Medhurst and
I have had a talk ; everything is smooth—
almost too smooth. I should like to have
snatched you out of the teeth of opposition,'
he said only half jestingly.

' Then shall I oppose you ?'

' No, no.   You must always be on my side.
I can't fight you.   Come now—the middle
of August ?'

There was a pause.

' Very well,' she said softly, and the next
moment he had drawn her head on his
shoulder.

' God bless you, my darling !   You know
how to give generously, like a true woman.'

' You'll be good to me ?'

' Will I not ?   How can I do enough ?'
Another pause.

' Henry !'

' My darling !'

' I do hate lectures.   I don't want to go to
any more.'

' Well, don't—don't go.   Say I've a personal objection to them, if you like.'

' So I will,' cried the girl joyfully.

' Lord Medhurst talked of returning to
Ashbury.'

Joan drew herself back, pale and startled.

'Oh no!'

'You wouldn't like it? Nor should I. It would be a hateful separation. It will be bad enough as it is, being able to get to you so seldom, but that would be worse, except—' he hesitated—'that there would be Saturdays and Sundays?'

'No, no!' said Joan imploringly. 'I would rather have the chance of the other days. Don't let papa do that. And—and—can't you come to some of the dances—late?'

He laughed.

'Not much use in that, except to look at you whirling round, and to wish the other fellow at the bottom of the sea. Perhaps now you won't be very keen about going?'

'Oh, why not?' she said quickly.

'Why not? Well, after all, why not? I expect I'm no judge, and it's natural enough when you're in the crowd to do like the rest of the crowd. But we'll get out of

it all by-and-by, Joan. We'll find some
place as unlike London as possible, and be
happy.'

The young girl looked at him doubtfully.

'Can't you be happy in London?'

'I never knew what happiness was before,'
he said strongly.

'And all your work, all your interests are
here. I don't believe any other place would
suit you as well.'

'Perhaps not. It's good of you, at any rate,
to think of me. But you, my country bird,
how will you bear it?'

She smiled at him.

'Oh, very well.'

He flattered himself that this meant that
she could be content where he was, and felt
blissfully grateful.

'And you would rather remain here now
—you can give up Ashbury?'

'Oh yes, we must stay! Besides——'

'What?'

' If we are to be married in August, I shall have hundreds of things to get.'

' Is that really a necessary part of the performance ? I'm sure you look to me as if you had hundreds of things already.'

' Oh !' cried Joan indignantly, ' I have nothing—nothing like other girls !'

' Then you manage to look twenty times better.'

' That may be,' she said, nodding her pretty head ; ' but I like nice things.'

' And you shall always have them.'

In this fashion he was ready to promise anything, everything—what will not a man undertake on the day when he gains the desire of his heart ?—and Joan went to her room very well pleased. She had talked before him of Lady Avonshire's ball, and her father and mother had said no word against it. Maria had somehow or other got an inkling of what had happened, and spoke to her with an added respect, refraining from her usual aggrieved remarks when Miss Joan tossed her dress in a crumpled heap on the floor. And the young girl fell asleep to dream that she was dancing a sort of fairy maze with Basil Gray.

What were Lancaster's thoughts as he walked away from Albion Street?

So long as it remained in sight, he turned round again and again to look at the house and bless his innocent darling. Though he had resolved to win her, now that she was won, it seemed the most wonderful thing possible that she should have given herself to him, and the man's great honest heart went out in a passion of love and devotion. He felt himself altogether unworthy of such a gift. How delicately sweet she was! how rude he seemed by her side! And yet, in spite of this contrast, which could not fail to present itself to her, she loved him—his breath came thick and short with the conviction that she loved him. She had not said so in so many words, it was true, but she had shown it by the looks which he had caught from her. And as he thought of all this with a tenderness, a reverence which could not be exceeded, his happiness was unbounded.

CHAPTER XVII.

ALL went smoothly with Lancaster's engagement. The one contrary thing about it was that he could see so little of Joan; for, as the end of the session approached, he was closely tied to the House, and was ready to declare that now, when he most wished for a little liberty, he was less than ever able to take it. But this was a comparatively small matter, and only caused him to look forward with greater longing to the time when she would be all his own. The wedding would be at Ashbury, and with the help of her lover Joan had carried her point, and was to stay in London until towards the end of July.

She had carried her point, and by dint of a free interpretation of his wishes, which she did not hesitate to advance when she considered it necessary, she contrived to carry many other points. Yet she was not really satisfied. Say what she would, her father and mother would not always yield, or allow her to be the free agent she expected to find herself. They remonstrated with her for caring so much for balls which Lancaster could not attend, and now and then refused to let her go. Nor, when there, had she the freedom she anticipated. On the contrary, it sometimes appeared that they felt themselves compelled to watch her with more extreme care than before. With regard to her trousseau she was allowed a fairly free hand; but even there Lady Medhurst would not tolerate anything in the form of extravagance. For these reasons she looked forward eagerly to the time when she would be married, and only obliged to account to Lancaster, who she felt sure would be her slave.

The greatest astonishment had been caused by the announcement of the engagement. Lancaster, the woman-hater—Lancaster, the unfruitful theme of many a supposition—Lancaster, who, if ever he married, was to marry Lady Millicent Fairlie—that this Benedick, this most improbable of wooers, should have fallen a victim to the charms of the youngest beauty, and succumbed at once—all this was the cause of an immense amount of talk. Nor were there wanting those who were equally amazed that she should have accepted him, and prognosticated that a marriage of two persons so unlike in appearance and in character could bring nothing but disaster.

The Ashtons were as much amazed as anyone. Even Elizabeth had not been able to believe that Sir Henry's had been more than a passing tribute of admiration, from which he would return to Millicent. She would scarcely have credited it if Lady Medhurst had not herself brought the news.

'Joan—Joan going to marry Sir Henry Lancaster!' exclaimed Mrs. Ashton. 'Is it possible? And are you pleased? Medhurst would like it, I am sure; but you— I don't know—he seems the very opposite of Joan, though, of course, he is everything that could be desired. My dear Emily, you have taken away my breath!'

'We were all more or less astonished, to tell the honest truth,' said Lady Medhurst calmly; 'but that does not prevent our feeling really rejoiced that the child should have made such a choice.'

'She is a very beautiful girl,' said Mrs. Ashton with warmth.

'She has met with a good deal of admiration—so much as often to make me uneasy— and her father feels that she will now be in the best possible hands.'

'Oh, I can understand all that; I can understand your being pleased. My wonder has only been that Sir Henry should be the sort of man to attract a young girl like Joan. But one never knows,' added Mrs. Ashton with a sigh, 'and, indeed, I congratulate you very heartily, Nan'—as her daughter came into the room—'here is a piece of news for you !'

Nan was also astonished, if not so sincerely.

'Sir Henry Lancaster ! Not really !' she exclaimed. 'When can he have found time to make love ?'

'He has certainly not wasted any of his opportunities; he has even managed to do a very pretty thing,' said Lady Medhurst, 'for he found out that Joan was fretting over an accident which has happened to our old weeding-woman—a great favourite with us all—and he went down to Ashbury to see and to bring news of her back to Joan.'

' I call that very nice,' said Mrs. Ashton.

' When was this ?' asked Nan.

' The day before the wedding, and on the day itself——'

' He got his reward ? Well, I shall tell Joan that she's a sly little puss, coming up to London so shy and terrified that she blushed if she was looked at, and now carrying off the man of all others who was supposed to be fascination-proof. Doing it so quietly, too! How on earth he can have found a square inch on which to propose in the middle of that crush, I can't conceive ! It only shows that he is a very determined man.'

' Joan was missing, if you remember,' said Lady Medhurst, not sorry to explain her daughter's small escapade.

' And now do you go back to Ashbury ? I suppose she will not mind giving up the rest of the season ?' asked Mrs. Ashton.

' She wishes to stay on, and perhaps, as there are all her things to get, it is as well that we should.   The wedding is to be in August. Of course, that is rather sooner than one would have desired, but it will enable them to go abroad, and later in the year Sir Henry will be tied by meetings and political duties, so that his wish for an early date is reasonable.'

When Nan retailed this conversation to her sister, Elizabeth burst out :

'Horrid, horrid man !   But he will be punished — I am quite sure he will be punished !   He has just been blinded by a pretty face ; he thinks she is all simplicity and sweetness, and that he will be able to mould her.   Mould her !   That is what men like Sir Henry think such a delightful occupation ; they haven't the common-sense to see that by the time a girl has grown up she is pretty well moulded.   Dress, gaiety, flattery —there isn't a thing which Sir Henry hates which she doesn't love.'

'I have an idea that she can flirt,' said Nan.

'Flirt ? Of course she can—and will. And Millicent would have made such a good wife !'

' Well, we can't force man—or even woman—to marry where we wish,' returned Nan, lazily philosophical. ' I am very sorry about Millicent, but I think it will be rather amusing if Joan leads him a dance. Heigh-ho ! I suppose we shall have to be brides-maids ?'

' Oh, don't ! I thought at least we should be free of weddings for a time. I am sick of the word.'

' Elizabeth, don't be misanthropical. What colour shall I suggest for the bridesmaids' dresses ? Our cousin is sure to come to me for counsel.'

' Is she ?' with a laugh.

' I think they had better be white—clear white—and apricot,' pursued Nan, calmly resolute. ' That will suit me very well, and will be as good as anything you could have. I shall tell her those must be the colours.'

Tell her she might, and did, but Joan only smiled and said she had not thought much about the matter. If Nan had but known, there was not the smallest chance of the young lady making over to another that or any other decision which it pleased her to keep in her own hands, and no one felt more enjoyment than she in dwelling upon details which Lady Medhurst would have dismissed with a word. That everything should be good and simple was Joan's mother's creed ; it did not at all content Joan, who was always pleading the difference of her position.

' You are so young !' said the mother.

' I shall be just as much married as if I were older, and I shall be expected to have everything of the best because of being his wife.'

' Are you sure you are thinking of him ?' said Lady Medhurst once, but Joan only opened her eyes and smiled.

If Lady Medhurst—who did not possess

extraordinary discernment — was at times troubled by a shade of uneasiness, her misgivings were not shared by her husband. He was serenely gratified. The little cloud which for a moment had rested on his system, that sudden, amazing, momentary revolt of Joan, he had, upon consideration, put down to not unnatural excitement, to his daughter having been thrown off her balance by an unexpected event, and had therefore dismissed it from his mind. Having always been keenly alive to his responsibilities with regard to his daughter's training, he was now cheerfully prepared to make them over to Lancaster; the curious part was that he seemed to be unaware that the person to whom they most belonged was Joan herself. It was perfectly true that he thought of her still as a child, whose privileges must be very carefully fenced about. Lancaster, who saw her before him as a beautiful girl, never realized how complete this fencing had been or what it was to her to find herself without it.

Less still could he have realized that she looked upon him chiefly as a means of doing away with it.

To him she was so much! His first love, brought to him at an age when most men have run through the course of two or three loves. It is hard to satisfy the demands of a sober judgment and high ideals, and hitherto these characteristics had kept Lancaster's heart his own; but he was but a foolish body after all to have provoked Dan Cupid into wrath with certain scoffs and ironical jests of his upon other of his friends who had fallen easier victims. In an unguarded moment the young rascal had slipped on the bandage, and where were his judgment and his ideals now? Just as silly as the rest of him—singing the praise of the sweetest, the loveliest, the dearest!

For to him she was all these. And it was

a constant marvel to him that, being what she was, she could yet give her heart to him. He wondered at it ; he wondered at his own audacity in winning her ; sometimes he caught sight of himself by the side of this dainty beautiful creature, and was struck with sudden amazement at the contrast.

Lord Waterton had been the most astonished of those who wondered over the engagement, and it must also be owned that he was secretly disappointed. He had liked Lancaster ; he had fancied that Millicent liked him ; and if he must have a son-in-law at all, here was the one he would have chosen. But as his principles were in this matter very much at war with his inclinations, and he really dreaded the moment when he should give away his daughter, he was easily consoled, and, when he had watched Millicent for a while and saw no change in her, allowed himself to feel relieved, and was for some time in unusually good spirits.

No one, not even Elizabeth Ashton,
ventured to allude to Lady Millicent's own
feelings, for in spite of her gentleness there
was a certain reserve behind which, when
she intrenched herself. there was no penetrat-
ing. And, indeed, with her the sharpest
pangs had been endured before she went
down to Denningham, her sensitiveness
having quickly shown her the change in
Lancaster. He had intended to be the first
to tell her of his engagement, for he still
clung to her friendship ; but happily for her,
rumour was before him, and she was spared
the agony of hearing it from his own lips.
When he came at last, others were there,
and her few words of congratulation required
to be quickly spoken, and as briefly answered.
He stayed but a short time, and when he
had departed the talk naturally fell upon his
intended marriage.

' He managed to spring it upon the world
very cleverly,' said a shrewd impatient-look-

ing lady. 'I must say I like anyone who contrives to give one a surprise. Tell me this, Lady Millicent, were you as much astonished as the rest of us?'

Lady Millicent appeared to reflect for a moment.

'I don't think I was. I had my suspicions.'

'Well, is it a good choice? Will she suit him?'

'Ah, that I can't say. I don't see why she shouldn't; there is something about her which is most attractive.'

'I was prepared to hear that that handsome, good-for-nothing Basil Gray had made another hit,' put in old Lady Netley. 'I suppose her father would have sent him to Coventry; but, upon my word, he's so amusing and brisk, I don't wonder at any girl losing her heart to him. At Hurlingham, the other day, there was no one half so pleasant. Oh, were you there, Major Lascelles? Well, you didn't come and talk to me, so you mustn't expect to have pretty things said of you.'

' I couldn't pretend to rival Gray,' said the young man.

' No. When he is agreeable, there's nothing so agreeable as a scapegrace. That's what made me think it possible that Basil Gray might cut out Sir Henry Lancaster. But weight—good solid weight—has carried the day.'

' They say he is very much in love,' said the first speaker.

' I am sure he is,' Lady Millicent said quietly.

' But is she ? That's half the question, at any rate,' returned Lady Netley, rising. When she was in her brougham she said to her daughter : ' Now there's an instance of endurance. I've always said that nothing could exceed the cool heroism of a well-born woman, and Millicent Fairlie is a case in point. Not the quiver of an eyelid—not a touch of acidity in her words; and all the while—oh, poor thing, she was feeling!'

'If she didn't show it, how do you know, mother?' inquired her daughter, a sandy and rather dull young woman.

'Because I've still got a heart, my dear. It is very well covered up and hidden away, on the whole, but every now and then it has something to say and manages to say it. It can even ache a little, though you mightn't believe it, and it ached to-day. She's brave, she's brave; she's got the spirit of her ancestors. I suppose that will stick to us longer than plate or pictures—at any rate, it can't be put up at Christie's, or I wouldn't say much for its chances.'

Basil Gray, when the news reached him, took it good-naturedly enough, and carried it down to Roehampton. He laughed a good deal at Lancaster, and he said nothing of his own failure.

'Well,' said his mother, 'I am disappointed,

I confess. If you had only made up your mind more quickly, Basil, Henry would have had no chance. What can she see in Henry ?'

'She sees money,' said Gray, tossing a bunch of cherries into Sissy's fat little up-turned hands. 'I wish I saw a little more of the same article. I'm awfully hard up, as you mayn't be surprised to hear ; and, upon my word, I don't know how the money goes ; I don't spend much, I vow. The fact is, it's all wasted upon bills. Can you think of any-one likely to leave me a legacy ? If you could, I'd go and call upon her—it must be a she—every day. I'd even stay with a maiden aunt. But I haven't got a maiden aunt, have I ?'

'Old Miss Gray.'

'Oh, she's a Gray. There's no coming over a Gray. Mary's a Gray. Sis, did you ever get your aunt to do anything foolish ?'

Sissy looked reflective, but she was too

much occupied with a large cherry to answer.

' I don't know that I very much regret this marriage. after all,' said Mrs. Gray cheerfully. ' She is excessively pretty, but I doubt her having much in her.'

' Perhaps enough to balance me,' said her son, with a laugh. ' Well, mother, I shall get out of London while I've got the money to pay the fare. Yachting's as cheap an amusement as any when you yacht at another man's expense ; and Tom Hunter has asked me to cruise about a bit with him, so I'll go. Do you approve, Mary ? Don't you think I'm growing economical ?'

Apparently his ideas of economy were not the same as his sister's. She tried, however, to smile a little.

' It will be charming if you are.'

' I am, really ; and you ought to encourage me. I shall be ever so much better out of London—if I can go,' he added significantly.

26—2

Mary's compact little features changed. His mother exclaimed :

'Oh, Basil !'

'Couldn't help it, I give you my word. London's an awful place for making money fly. I don't understand it. I've been so screwy—there are half a dozen poor devils I'm ashamed to see. It's the coming home, and having so many things to get—don't you see ?'

'Yes, I see—I see,' said his mother sympathetically ; 'that Cape business was a mistake from beginning to end, and led to nothing but expense. I hope the next thing you get will be in your own country. You must make that a condition.'

'Yes, I will,' said Basil, looking at his sister with a laugh. 'Sis, you don't happen to have any ready money about you that you could manage to lend your old dad, have you ?'

'Do you want some money ?' said Sissy,

promptly thrusting a cherry-stained hand into her pocket. 'I've dot twopence.'

'No, no; keep your riches, Sis—if you can,' hastily. He extracted a sixpence from his own waistcoat-pocket, and tossed it to her. 'There! add that to the store.'

Mrs. Gray got up and went to her writing-table.

'Mary,' she said, 'we must do something for him, poor boy! Is my cheque-book in the drawer? Ah, there is Mary looking disapproving. She thinks us both dreadfully young and inconsiderate; but, as I tell her, if I live to be a hundred I hope I shall never become a slave to money. What can it do, except be of use? Mary makes herself miserable, and I—I don't trouble my head about it. We haven't got much, but it's always enough. There, Basil,' she added, signing her name with a flourish, 'I wish it were twenty times as much, my dear boy.'

'I won't come on you again, mother,' he

said, pocketing the cheque with—to do him justice—something of a shamefaced air. 'I shall be on the look-out for something, and when I've got it, this shall come back to you; for it's only a loan, recollect. I wouldn't take it otherwise.'

Mary had made no open remonstrance; she sat looking down at her plate, holding her hands tightly clasped. As Basil said this she got up quickly. 'Come, Sissy!' she said, in a voice which sounded strained.

'I want to stay with daddy,' said Sissy, scrambling off her chair backwards, and trotting round the table to her father.

'No, no,' he said; 'be a good girl and go to your aunt.'

He carried her to the door, put her down outside, and shut the door between them as she began to cry.

'Mary will soon quiet her,' said Mrs. Gray as he returned. 'Poor Mary! I wish she could learn to take life more easily.'

CHAPTER XVIII.

SOME cynic has said that the most humiliating study in human nature is that of a sensible man in love. Cynicism is seldom trustworthy. When it is genuine it springs out of a sour soil of disappointments and heart-burnings, and when—as is more often the case—it is assumed, it is intended to cover the poverty of actual growth by a showy mockery of what is better than itself. Depend upon it the man who made that assertion either had a successful rival, or was not worthy the affection of a good woman, and so fell back upon a sneer. But I am bound to own that, if it is not humiliating, there is a certain monotony in it

—one human being being so remarkably like
another; and Sir Henry Lancaster, the rising
man of his party, showed himself, in the
interval, the short interval of his engagement,
in every way so similar to others that there
is not much to be said about him.   He was
very happy, and the moments he snatched to
spend with his love were the sweetest he had
ever known.   What man is not the better for
such moments and such sweetnesses?

After the Medhursts left London, Lancaster
went down on Saturdays and spent the Sundays with them.   Here, indeed, were white
days.   To walk with Joan down the steep
lane which led to the little church, where the
arching hawthorn-trees grew tall overhead; to
stop with her at the half-way gate and look
across the closely-cut field upon the scattered
hamlet below, through which flowed the river
like a silver streak, while overhead white
clouds were tossed by the wind upon a blue
summer sky, and the larks, high up, were

singing to the sun; to wait there while the
children, a rosy-faced little procession, came
trooping down the lane from school, clasping
their prayer-books and their pocket-handker-
chiefs, and their hot little bunches of flowers,
and staring at Miss Joan and the gentleman
Miss Joan was going to wed—and the old
men came touching their hats, and the old
women making their curtseys, and all turned
in at the little white churchyard gate, and
walked between that silent company of the
dead, among whom some of them would soon
lie down and rest; to follow when the bell
had changed to its five minutes' call, and,
passing through the rude porch, go down a
step or two, and so up the church to the
chancel where Lord and Lady Medhurst
were already seated. The peacefulness, the
quiet of it all, attracted Lancaster greatly.
He liked the country faces, the fine heads of
some of the old men, the effect of the sunshine striking in here and there through the

perpendicular windows, the simplicity of the singing. Best of all he liked to know that Joan, his Joan, was close to him, and that here in a very little while she would give herself to him altogether. He knelt down and prayed God bless her.

In the afternoon they went to see Martha and Thomas. Martha was not dying, but it scarcely seemed likely that she would get about again, and she was as querulous as Thomas was philosophical.

'Thomas med know that 'tes different vur he,' she lamented; 'he's been here so long, an' hev got no weeds on his moind. That thyarr bwoy of Martha Gay's that Mr. Andrews hev putt in, what doos he know? They've no reason between 'em, those bwoys, an' doos more harm than good. Can't do no harm in the shrubbery, Miss Joan? You wait an' see what zort of a pleäce Martha Gay's bwoy makes of 'en.'

'She's quite changed; she isn't the same

Martha,' cried Joan impatiently, when they
came out. 'She's worse than old Thomas
ever was. And she used to be so nice. I
can't think why people can't be contented.
Poor old thing, that's what she always said
of Thomas,' she added with a laugh. 'I
thought she'd have wanted to know all about
my things, but she doesn't seem to care for
anything. She's quite changed.'

'She shall never want,' said Lancaster
compassionately.

'Oh, mamma will see to her,' the young
girl returned.

'Do you know,' he said in a low voice,
'that when I come here and see what you
are giving up, this beautiful life in such a
country, among the people who love you—
and whom you love—and when I remember
that it is for me, I feel as if all I can do is a
mere nothing. If you regret it, if London
wearies you, what shall I do?'

Joan looked at him with her delicious smile.

'London won't weary me ; I like it,' she said softly.

'Oh, well, you say that, I know, to make me happy. We shall be out of it, at any rate, for some time. I wonder what you will say to Switzerland ? But I'm not afraid about that — you're sure to admire it. And though this time of year is really the worst time imaginable, and tourists will be swarming all over the place, yet I think we can manage to dodge them.'

'How ?' asked the girl quickly. 'Remember I want to see all the places that everybody sees. It's so annoying when people ask you where you've been, to have to own yourself an ignoramus.'

The difference there is in a sentiment according to the person that utters it ! For what was this but that atrocious reason for travel, the seeing what other people have seen, which Sir Henry had often been remorselessly down upon ? And yet—now—

he never even realized it. It seemed to him the most natural and the most praiseworthy reason possible.

'Of course you shall see them,' he said; 'and I'll tell you how I mean to manage. But, look here, we're going up to the windmill, aren't we? If you'll wait a minute, I'll go to the house and bring down Jack and Jill, and little Moth. It's a shame they shouldn't have a walk.'

And in a minute or two there was a wild joyous chorus of barks and yelps and a rush of excited dogs out of the gate, the collies tumbling over each other, and Moth, a small silver-gray Skye, with long feathery wing-like ears, which had gained him his name, flying after them full tilt. It took a little time for these new companions to settle down to comparative calm, and then Lancaster went on with his plan of travel, to which Joan listened more anxiously than he guessed.

' Yes,' he said, ' you shall see the places ; I can well understand that you would like them

to be something more to you than mere
names, and, of course, the very fact of all
those people buzzing about them is owing to
their having gained such a reputation for
beauty.   But as I was saying, there are ways
of evading the crowd.   I know the parts
where we shall go pretty tolerably, and I
know a good number of snug little places just
off the beaten track, or on it, only not where
people generally stop—you won't mind a
little roughing it. will you?'

'No,' said Joan blankly.   'But I think, I
am very much afraid, the maid will mind.'

'Oh, we can easily get rid of her,' he
remarked with great cheerfulness.   'We can
send her on to the next halting-place, or—oh,
I'll dispose of her.   It will be such a blessing
to be out of the reach of *tables d'hôte ;* we
shall get good food, trout and plain things,
and the people are first-rate—they'll do anything for those they like.   You'll have a fine
time with them.'

'I think a *table d'hôte* would be new and amusing,' said the girl, and there was just a touch of petulance in her tone.

But he did not notice it.

'You'll be tired to death of them in a week. I know you, my little wild girl. I know what you'll like—the riding, and the scrambling, and the flowers—though the flowers will be pretty well over—and the little streams that rush along in wooden troughs, and the solitude of the great mountains.'

A pause.

'How long shall we be there?'

'I'm afraid we must be home by the end of September. But, after all, by that time the days grow short and the evenings chilly, and you'll not be sorry to turn homewards.

Sorry?—no. And he little thought that she was saying to herself:

'Five or six weeks will soon be over, and when I am out there I dare say I shall be able to avoid those horrid lonely places.'

He went on :

'As for me, go where I will, I don't believe I shall see anything I like better than
this.'

' Than this !' repeated Joan, staring. Yet
Lancaster had some reason for his admiration,
for rain had fallen the night before and
freshened all the somewhat russet-green of
July, and the beautiful undulating common
could not have been more rich in colour than
it was now, with the heather coming out, and
with golden gleams of gravel under the dark
peat. To the south it lost itself in blue distances of wood, fading into palest colour of
far-away sea-mists ; but on the other side it
swept boldly up, flinging off its sheltering
trees, and running along sharp and distinct
against a background of white sky, until the
windmill crowned its summit. And but for the
dogs, which were in full excitement of rabbit-
hunting, and the song of the larks, and the
constant changing and intermingling of the

dazzling clouds, it was all absolutely solitary
and silent and still——

'And slow,' said the girl, going on with her
own mute comments. 'Oh, I hope, I *hope*
he won't be always trying to get to this sort
of place! But he can't! That is such a
comfort: he must live in the midst of things
and people. Only I've always got to wait.
I'm sure I don't want very much, but I never
meant to marry a hermit, and nothing,
nothing shall induce me to give way——'

'And she,' he was thinking—'what it will
be to have her as now, away from that rush
of fevered life, where there is so much to bewilder and excite her? She is so innocent
and so sweet that the simple pleasures are
those to which she will most gladly turn; she
is different from all other women'—yes, this
clever, shrewd politician, whose business it
was to read the characters of men and nations,
was deluded enough to allow himself to be
dragged to this pitch of fatuity—'and will

not trouble herself about the things for which they are ready to sell their souls——'

'We must go through Paris, and come home that way, too,' said her thoughts. 'That's one comfort—no cross-country cuts for me! And there I can get a good heap of things which mamma won't let me have now, and they shall all be the very latest fashions. Oh, delightful! After all, it's rather nice to be married; yes, indeed, I mean it to be very nice——'

'Well,' he said aloud, looking at her and smiling, 'a penny for your thoughts.'

She laughed and shook her head.

'I shall find them out, I warn you. I know something about cross-examination. You looked very happy—were you thinking of Ashbury?'

'No—oh no!'

'Then '—in a low voice—' of me?'

'Perhaps—perhaps not,' she replied saucily. 'Don't imagine that you will always have your own way. I've got a will as well as you.'

There was a pause; then:

'Look here, Joan,' he said simply, 'I'm sometimes afraid that I have fallen into a domineering, hectoring sort of a way. I don't suppose I shall be such a brute as to domineer over you, but nobody knows where habit may lead one, and—don't you stand it. Just pull me up sharp, will you?'

If any of those men who were accustomed to listen to the trenchant words which fell from Sir Henry could have heard this meek request! But Joan took it very contentedly.

'Oh yes,' she said. 'You know you promised to be good to me.'

After this, perhaps for the sake of the self-respect of mankind, more had better not be recorded. It is certain that he fell very low indeed in the abasement of his language, and that his hearer, the simple and innocent girl who was so infinitely more free from the

wicked wiles of the world than any other
woman, accepted it all without surprise, as
no more than her due.

That to him was an idyllic day. He
never lost the impression of its bliss. Coming
home, they left the sterner outlines of the
common behind them, and set their faces
towards those soft blue distances where all
outline melted into a kind of aërial enchant-
ment.   The dogs ran in and out of the
prickly gorse and heather, little Moth
sturdily following his big companions ; the
white clouds cleared away, and the sky took
a delicate and indescribable brightness.
What did it matter that Lord Medhurst
was waiting for them at the gate, watch in
hand, scandalized with the fear that one of
his family should be too late for church ?
The dogs were left at the lodge ; the little
party walked quickly down the steep lane,
across which the hedge shadows were flinging themselves. And now the larks were

mute, but the air was sweet with honey-
suckle, the rooks were cawing, and the not
unmusical clang of the little church-bell
vibrated upon the stillness.

When they came out again, Lady Medhurst, who had been sent off earlier, took
away her husband, and Lancaster got Joan
to linger behind. The lane had lost its
sunshine charm by this time, it was all in
shadow ; only the thick masses of the haw-
thorn stood up dark against what seemed
as if it must be a marvellously clear and
radiant sky. But it was not until they had
reached the top of the hill, and all the west
lay spread before them, that the cause of
this gracious radiance was discovered. For
the sun was sinking in such glory as if he
were celebrating a triumph—a central blaze
of living light—and across this were bars
of yet keener, more unapproachable light,
with a precipice of purple cloud on one side,
as if a mountain had been riven asunder to

let the glory through. The precipice itself was edged with the marvellous gold, while on the other side great tawny rays rushed upwards and melted into a delicate dusky light, and across this were flying obliquely a troop of the most exquisite cool gray clouds, broken into loveliest shape, and momentarily forming fresh combinations. Underneath this splendid pageant, earth and woods lay in sober russet, as if they dared not move or speak while it was going on, and except for the blue smoke curling up from unseen cottages, there was no sign of human life about.

For the moment Joan's petty fancies were swallowed up in the yearning which such a sight stirs in immortal souls, and as Lancaster turned and kissed her, she felt as if she really loved him.

A few days later they were married.

CHAPTER XIX.

WELL, they were away in the land of snows, and flowers, and tinkling cow-bells. London was empty. It is true that a million or so of people were just keeping it inhabited, so to speak; but they made hardly any impression on the vacant spaces. It was possible to stroll across Piccadilly or Bond Street without needing to trouble yourself about passing vehicles. The rectors of the fashionable churches had left their services to curates; the great doctors had fled; and if a considerable number of those who attended the churches, or employed the doctors, were still in town, they did not put themselves

en evidence, but allowed the social fetters
to drop off, wore their old clothes, and would
not do each other the wrong of supposing
that they were there to be called upon.

The Ashtons had not gone abroad.
Marrying a daughter is apt to run away
with spare cash, and they had merely returned to their house near Winchester,
where Mrs. Ashton was quite happy over
a scheme for bringing down sickly children
from London, and boarding them at different
cottages. Elizabeth and Nan had been two
of Joan's bridesmaids; but no choice of
colour had fallen to Nan; Joan had decided
it all, and, it must be said, with success.
Immediately after the wedding, Elizabeth
went to Denningham, to stay with Lady
Millicent.

She had at first abstained from talking
about the marriage, which had just taken
place, from an instinctive dread of wounding
her friend. Nothing had ever passed be-

tween them which touched on a supposed
liking between Lady Millicent and Sir
Henry; first, because nothing had been
sufficiently definite to cause such a confidence ; and secondly, because Lady Millicent was not a person to require a confidante.
Elizabeth, with her apparent touch of hardness, really needed one more. And now, as
soon as Millicent discovered that there was
a slight holding back, an avoidance of the
subject, she quietly led the conversation in
that direction, and asked many questions.

'Oh, Medhurst is very much pleased !
Naturally, he feels it to be such a credit
to his bringing up,' returned Elizabeth.
The two friends were strolling round a very
charming, sheltered little garden—a nook in
the midst of other gardens—in which the
turf was finer, and the flowers more brilliant,
than elsewhere, and Millicent was gathering
a great bunch of carnations. 'I wish Medhurst weren't such an excellent man, so that

one might be allowed the joy of saying something against him.'

' But, Joan ! Did she look her prettiest ?'

' Yes,' the other admitted reluctantly ; ' she did.'

' Elizabeth,' said Lady Millicent quietly, ' you're prejudiced—you're not fair upon Joan.'

' Well, I don't like her.'

' Why ?'

' Because I'm prejudiced, as you say, I suppose,' said Elizabeth, with a smile. ' Why don't I like her ? Let me see. Well, I think she will put her own pleasure first ; and I think she will get her way by crooked means if she can't by straight ; and I think she will always have some shabby little excuse ready when she wants it ; and I think, as you said, that I am really unfair. So there's an end of it.'

' Remember,' said the other, disregarding this flourish, ' that the sudden change was

enough to turn her head. Snubbed all her
life, conscientiously snubbed, and then
plunged with that beauty into a world which
couldn't find enough to say about her—you
and I, Elizabeth, have never gone through
such an ordeal.'

'Well, she wasn't shy, though we were all
under the impression that she was.'

'No, she wasn't shy, but she was timid,
self-conscious and timid, and when she is out
of the atmosphere of Lord Medhurst's constant remarks, I believe she will shake off
her fear. I am sure she will, if——'

She paused.

'If?'

'If she loves her husband,' said Lady
Millicent with a slight effort. 'He is large-
minded, and small petty motives seem to
wither up in his presence. I don't know how
it might have been if she had married one
of those young men who were buzzing about
her.'

'Basil Gray, for instance!' interrupted Elizabeth bitterly.

'Yes, Mr. Gray,' agreed the other quietly. 'Was that likely?'

Elizabeth had turned away to gather a piece of jessamine. She faced round suddenly.

'Millicent—did you ever know?'

'I guessed—something.'

'I never talked to you about it—I talked to no one.'

'No.'

'It wasn't anything to boast about.'

'Or to be ashamed of,' said the other girl, kissing her. 'My poor dear!'

'I don't know—I'm ashamed now. And I wanted just to say that I think it is this which makes me unfair to Joan—I'm not good, I'm not unselfish, and when I saw him drawn away to her, I believe I hated her. He does not spare me at any rate. And yet —if he were to come back to-morrow——'

'Would you marry him?' asked Millicent softly.

'Luckily, perhaps, I couldn't,' said Elizabeth with a hard laugh. 'Having nothing to live upon does sometimes set up a barrier to folly; but if anybody were to do me the mischief of leaving me a fortune, I suppose that folly would ride triumphant. You couldn't do that, could you, Millicent?' As her friend did not answer she went on: 'But I know you couldn't. People talk of my pride, just because I've a sort of fierce air about me. Little they know that it is you—fragile, gentle you—who would die and make no sign. And as for Basil, I don't really think that it would enter his head that all which had happened could be the smallest reason for—for things not being as he once wished if he wished it again. He has not the faintest sense of responsibility.'

'Oh, Elizabeth!'

'Yes, you wonder that I can see all that,

and yet care for him. But I do. I read all his faults only too plainly. I see weaknesses which other people don't see. I know quite well what he is going to do. And yet I'm fool enough to love him.'

' Does——' Millicent hesitated.

' Does he love me, were you going to ask ? Yes—as much as he loves other people, as much as he can ever love anyone. If he married he would be a good husband; he is very affectionate. Now, about Joan, for instance, it was extremely silly, but I understand. He was not in love with her, but he admired her very much, and instead of reflecting that Medhurst would have nothing to say to a penniless man, it amused him to try to play upon Medhurst's foibles, and his imagination led him to suppose that he could persuade him to get him some appointment and to give him his daughter. It would not really enter his head that Joan might suffer if this rose-coloured scheme failed.'

'Oh,' said Millicent gravely, 'but this makes him dangerous. If he only thinks of himself!'

'He is dangerous,' Elizabeth agreed. 'Joan's heart is a little behind her mistress; it has not yet asserted itself, but if Basil were to get hold of it, things might go ill. There is one safeguard, however, for her. I mean in probable events.'

'What ?'

'That he can't go on long. I suppose in a very little while he will have spent all his money, if he hasn't done it already, and then —well, then he can hardly be quite so much to the fore as he has been.' The two girls were by this time strolling across the park towards a silver sheet of water, which went by the name of the pond, and anyone looking at Elizabeth Ashton would have seen that she was walking very erectly, with her hands tightly clenched, and her head turned away from her companion. 'That is the best thing which can happen,' she went on.

And what could Lady Millicent say? For this is a sore which no kind touch can soothe. Separation—death itself—have not the bitterness which belongs to an unworthy love.

' Dear——' she began, and then stopped.

' The best thing which can happen,' repeated Elizabeth loftily. And she even turned her eyes upon her friend, perhaps hardly knowing how wet they were with tears.

' Do you suppose,' the other girl said hastily, ' that if he had another chance he might do better? Because if I were to ask papa, he would try. There is nothing really against him, is there?' she asked in a lower voice.

' No,' said Elizabeth. ' But he will not do better. He will never change. You need not waste your kind thoughts upon me, Millicent. The one saving point in my folly is that I know all about it, and don't deceive myself. What he is, Basil Gray has been

from his childhood, and will be till his death.
And knowing what he is, and seeing the
harm he does in that airy irresponsible way
of his, I am yet fool enough——' She
broke down here, and dropped her face on
her hands. 'Oh,' she sobbed, 'I love him!
I love him!'

The passionate outcry went to her hearer's
heart.

'My poor Elizabeth!' she said mournfully,
and pulled down her hand, holding it tight in
hers, and laid her head lovingly against
Elizabeth's shoulder. By-and-by this mute
sympathy began to have its effect, and the
girl stopped her tears and made a proud
effort to smile and turn the subject.

'Do you know, Millicent,' she said, 'that I
like this spot the best of all the place?'

'Oh, and so do I,' said the other eagerly.
'There is the water to begin with—those
white stretches running out into the green
and breaking the reflections; and the sedges

where the moorhen has her nest; and all the beautiful long grasses just fringing the edge where the turf runs down. And don't you like the trees, and the tangled underwood, and the calm streaks of sunshine just falling here and there? Oh, I can tell you, Elizabeth, I have had many a battle royal over that undergrowth. Mr. West wants to clear it away, and is always declaring that it is bad for the trees. But so far I have managed to get papa on my side, and do tell him that you like it just as it is, and that you think it would be a thousand pities to alter it.'

It will be seen at once that this was a quick response to her friend's attempt, and that Lady Millicent talked on with the kindly intention of giving her time to recover herself altogether. But, indeed, what she said was very true, so far as the charm of this silent spot was concerned; and there could not have been a much more beautiful grouping of water and bank and trees. Then

they walked round to the other side and
caught a glimpse of the fine old house, with
the great oaks sweeping up on either side,
and the deer grouped not far away ; and
then Elizabeth must needs drag her hostess
to the boat-house and insist that they should
punt themselves out into the heart of those
green exquisite reflections and white reaches
of water, and no more was said about Basil
Gray, however much he may have remained
in their thoughts.

But the Lancaster marriage was not so
easily dismissed, for, from Sir Henry being a
public character, an acquaintance of Lord
Waterton's, and not unknown at Denningham, a good deal of interest was displayed
by the neighbourhood. Even at a school
treat Millicent was not safe from chance
allusions. In the midst of cutting bread
and butter, she found herself next Miss
Westcott, an excellent little woman, who did
the work of two curates, and had the small,

though amiable, weakness of desiring to know all about the affairs of her fellow-creatures. She had once met Sir Henry at the great house, and ever since had felt herself linked to State affairs. His marriage excited her greatly.

' I should so much have liked a peep at the bride,' she acknowledged; ' and I never wished so much before to be a mouse at a wedding. You know her, of course, Lady Millicent? And is she as beautiful as she is said to be?'

' She is very beautiful indeed.'

' Really! Well, now, I should hardly have thought that a man like Sir Henry would have cared so much about beauty. I should have expected him to have sought for more sterling qualities in his wife—though, to be sure, she may have those too, and it is very uncharitable of me to be so ready to suppose that she has not both. I think now we might cut some cake; the children don't get

cake like this anywhere else, Lady Millicent;
though what children are coming to, and
what they will expect next, I can't imagine!
But, you see, after meeting Sir Henry here,
one can't help feeling a great interest in him.
I am sure I always now read the debates,
though I used to think them so dull, just for
the hope of coming across something which
he has said ; and then, I can quite fancy his
saying it—I can almost see him.   I think he
is a person who impresses himself very much
upon you, don't you ?   It would not be at all
easy to forget him ?'

'No,' said Lady Millicent in a low voice,
'it would not be easy.'

'No ; that is what I have always said.   If
once you know him, I said, you can't put him
out of your mind.   Some people are quite
difficult to remember.   I am sure there was
that Mrs. Barr, the wife of one of the curates
—I dare say you recollect, he was the curate
who was so much liked, and who left only

last year; and yet when I try to recall what
Mrs. Barr was like, I can't succeed in the
very least. I can't even say what was the
colour of her hair. I wonder if she made a
greater impression upon you? I know she
was considered very amiable, and I often
blame myself for being so forgetful. But I
don't think I shall forget Sir Henry Lancaster to my dying day. Such a voice as he
had! I was always wishing one could hear
it in the pulpit. I am sure I hope he has a
good wife who will make him happy.'

'I hope so, too,' said Lady Millicent
earnestly. 'I don't think he was a man to
choose hastily.'

'Perhaps he will be bringing her here by-
and-by?' put in Miss Westcott with interest.
'Oh, Lady Millicent, I hope—I do hope you
haven't cut your hand!'

'Not quite—it was only a near escape. I
can't think how I can have been so stupid as
to let the knife slip!'

'And you look quite pale! I should not have talked so much and distracted your attention.'

'I don't think cake-cutting requires undivided attention,' said Lady Millicent, smiling; 'and I assure you that no harm is done. But ought the children to be peeping in at the tent? Aren't they supposed to be racing and jumping, and gaining voracious appetites?'

This was so altogether what Miss Westcott had ordained, that she was properly shocked by these stragglers having failed in their duty, and hurried off to insist upon their return to the larger flock. Other workers came running in to carry the loaded plates to the central table, and for a time everyone was too busy to think or speak of anything beyond the immediate business of the hour. The children filled two tents, and as the tables were decorated with fresh branches and great scarlet gladiolus, it all looked as gay and cheerful as possible. Millicent met Elizabeth hurrying along carrying a large white jug in both hands.

'Don't stop me,' she said ; ' I'm engaged in working out a problem. Do you see that round-faced boy ? He has had five cups of tea already, and he tells me he has only just begun. I am going to keep an exact account of how many he gets through.'

And it is to be feared that Elizabeth, from a desire for the marvellous, acted the part of a temptress on this occasion, for the small boy, by the time the repast was ended, presented a very sodden and flabby aspect, and declined to be annexed to any of the groups who were started for races, and for whom prizes dear to the heart of boys were provided, such as knives with ingenious nut-crackers and button-hooks attached. Also, Elizabeth ever after-wards asserted that on the occasion of a school-feast in Warwickshire she herself was called upon to pour out twelve cups of tea which were all drunk by one boy. And it is certain that she made a good deal of her story, whether it was statistically correct or not.

This was the sort of gathering where, considering the elements of which it was composed, it might have been reasonably expected that nothing was likely to be said about the Lancaster marriage, and yet, possibly from the same strange coincidence which, whenever we have a wounded limb, causes all blows and knocks to converge towards that spot, the subject seemed to crop up in the most unexpected manner. As Millicent was standing under a great wych-elm talking to the Vicar's wife, Lord Waterton came up, bringing a gentleman with him, whom he introduced as a Mr. Probyn.

'Curious thing, Millicent!' he said. 'Mr. Probyn's been asking whether Lancaster isn't a friend of ours. It seems he's in treaty for his house in Lennox Gardens. I'd no idea— had you?—that he had a house in view.'

'No,' said Millicent, 'no—I had heard nothing about it.'

'He is anxious to get mine,' said Mr. Probyn. 'To say the truth, I had not intended to turn out for another year; but Sir Henry got wind of its being in the market—through the agents, I expect—and he's been pressing me to let him have possession at once. He took a great fancy to the house. I suppose, being just married, he doesn't feel disposed to go through a second move.'

'Has he been over it?' asked Lord Waterton, with interest.

'That he has—most carefully. If he gives as much attention to the smaller details of his public department as he does in the matter of choosing a house, all I can say is that the State has a most valuable servant. But I hear that Lady Lancaster is very beautiful and very young, and that her husband is very much in love. Perhaps you can tell me, Lady Millicent, whether rumour is correct?'

'Quite correct,' said Lady Millicent, smell-

ing a rose which one of the children had
thrust into her hand. 'No one could well
be prettier than Lady Lancaster. Where
did you say your house was? Oh, Lennox
Gardens!—one of those pretty new houses?'

'Yes, the sunny side,' said Mr. Probyn,
gratified. 'I suppose I shall have to let him
have it, because one can't refuse a good offer
in these days; but I own I'm half sorry.
And I have told all my friends that I shouldn't
move for a year. But Sir Henry was so very
determined.'

'Determined? Well, look here, Mr.
Probyn,' said Lord Waterton, 'if it's any
consolation to you, you may take it as a certainty that you've got to do with the most
determined man in England. When once
Lancaster has set his mind on a thing, he'll
get it—mark my words.'

'So I have heard,' said Mr. Probyn, apparently deriving a little satisfaction from this
information. 'Some people say that is how
he gained his wife.'

'Oh, I don't know that,' Lord Waterton answered hastily. 'I don't see why that should be.'

'Well, he's not generally considered what is commonly called an attractive man,' returned the other ; 'and when a young beauty in her first season is carried off, people naturally discuss it.'

'But I think it unnecessary that they should do so,' said Lady Millicent, with a touch of dignity which made the Vicar's wife wonder what it was that had displeased her in Mr. Probyn. 'I think myself that it was the most natural thing in the world for Sir Henry Lancaster and his wife to fall in love with each other, and that we need not search for any hidden reason to explain it. Papa, have you spoken to Mr. Reed about the drum-and-fife band?'

And she left Mr. Probyn to be entertained by the Vicar's wife.

CHAPTER XX.

FOR the first week of her travels Joan enjoyed herself to the full. She felt as if she had broken her fetters, and there was a delightful sense of freedom—were it only from the thraldom of rigid punctuality — which exceeded all her light-hearted hopes. But there was yet more than this. For now, instead of being merely told when this, that, or the other was decided upon, her wishes appeared to be the pivot upon which the new order of things revolved. Her husband arranged everything with reference to them. The new maid had none of that air of familiarity which was

inseparable from Maria after long years of
service, and knowledge of Miss Joan in all
the phases of childhood, and girlhood, and
lessons, and letting down of frocks. Lady
Medhurst had heroically offered to resign
Maria to her daughter, but Joan would
have none of her, and, moreover, had resolved that if she did not altogether like the
new maid—her mother's choice—go she
should.

They stayed for a day or two in Paris,
and Joan was charmed. Lancaster pointed
out the famous buildings, and Joan made
a note of the shops where she intended to
spend a little money on her way home.
It made Lancaster so entirely happy to see
her keen enjoyment, that he never asked
himself what was really the source of this
enjoyment ; he only felt that it was delightful to feel her enthusiasms expanding, as it
were, under his guidance. She was always,
moreover, ready to fling some of them in

the direction he asked ; and Lord Medhurst's education had been solid enough for her to be really well informed in matters of history, so that she could respond with intelligence.

From Paris they went to Geneva, and Geneva again was not dull. So Chamounix. A great many people were travelling, and Joan liked to look at them, and liked still better to be looked at by them. Lancaster wished them all at Jericho, merely because he thought them an uninteresting, noisy crowd, and that Joan should endure them only seemed to him a farther proof of the kindness of her nature. He reflected with joy that he should soon escape from the throng ; he had the Eggischorn before him, and that, though in the way, was in a manner out of it, since people do not so much care to turn aside out of the track of railways or carriages, and, at any rate, there it would always be possible to wander away from them.

So they crossed the Tête Noire, and endured a night at Martigny, and the next day were bowling along the valley of the Rhone. And the day was so bright, the flowers in the meadows looked so gay, and the brown châlets made such pretty pictures standing up under their walnut-trees, that Joan could not but feel something of the charm. Nor was it lost when they reached Viesch, that picturesque jumble of wooden buildings, all gable and balconies. For the sun was still shining, and the balconies seemed made for bright bits of colour to hang themselves upon, and it all looked cheery enough. Better still, in Joan's eyes, a carriage was unloading at the door of the inn.

'Oh,' she cried joyfully, 'I do believe the Greshams have come, after all!'

Lancaster, who happened to be looking out on the other side, did not hear her exclamation, but he also had caught sight of the new arrivals. The Greshams were chief among those whom he desired to leave behind, and his disgust at beholding them was more than equal to his wife's glee.

'Oh, come,' he said, 'this is a nuisance! I thought, at any rate, we had disposed of those people. They said they were going to Zermatt, and I took all the care in the world not to breathe the name of Eggischorn in their hearing.' He looked doubtfully at his wife. 'I suppose you're too tired to push on farther?'

'Oh, much, much too tired!'

'And I don't know where we could push. Well, we must make the best of it, though I wish our friends were at the bottom of the sea,' he added with a laugh. 'You're not over-tired, are you, Joan? I haven't brought you too far?'

Then they got out, and in his new anxiety —for Joan had never before complained of

fatigue—Lancaster forgot the Greshams. He
recurred to them, however, presently, for
the little pine-wood inn was too small to
provide private sitting-rooms, and for dinner
it was necessary to go down to the *salle à
manger*.

'You will be their victim at once,' he said.
'I have noticed already that they showed an
inclination to make a prey of you, and, of
course, here, where there is hardly anyone
else, there will be no escape possible. Joan,
look here—I've an idea! This balcony isn't
so very small. Suppose we dine there, and
give them the slip altogether?'

But Joan shook her head with decision.

'It would be dreadfully squeezy,' she said,
'and I am sure you are much too big to sit
on a balcony. I should expect you to carry
it away altogether. No, no, let us go down,
and get what comfort we can in this funny
little hole. What harm can those poor
people do us?'

'Why, they can prevent us from having the world to ourselves,' he returned with comic indignation. 'Harm? I should think that was harm! And now, Joan, be serpent-wise, I implore you. Don't give them an inkling of our route, or how long we are going to stay, or—anything at all about us. I know that kind of family exactly. They haven't the brains to make out a plan for themselves, and so they track unfortunate victims like ourselves. How they found out we were coming here, I can't for the life of me imagine ; but you may be sure nothing else brought them. I don't believe they ever heard the name Eggischorn in their lives. They picked up our movements some-how.'

'Oh, how unreasonable you are!' interrupted Joan hastily. 'I dare say they laid their plans just as carefully as you. I dare say they could tell you about heaps of nice places! Mr. Gresham told me that his father and mother came abroad every year.'

'Has that young cub been talking to you?' said Lancaster, smiling, but pushing up his under-lip.

'Oh, a few words!' said the girl lightly. 'When you turn yourself into a bear, I'm obliged to be the more civil, you know.'

'I believe I am a bear sometimes,' he acknowledged remorsefully; 'but if anyone can tame me it will be you.'

She went up to him, and lifted her face to his with a smile.

'Yes; I shall get you quite nice and civil before we go home,' she announced; and anyone looking on might have read a little triumph in her eyes as he released her. 'And now, to begin with, we will go down, and you must be good to the poor Greshams, and not look at them as if you wished to bite, and not be ungracious when they talk to you about their plans——'

'But we won't let them know where we are going !' he cried in much alarm.

'Oh, there is no occasion for that,' returned she indifferently.

And when they went down, it must be said for Lancaster that he was very careful to profit by his lesson. He spoke quite amiably to the Greshams, and said nothing deprecia- tory about the accommodation or the probable discomforts awaiting travellers in that par- ticular part of the country. He did not even conceal that they were intending to go up to the little hotel on the Eggischorn, and, indeed, as no one is likely to halt at Viesch who has not that point in view, it might have been difficult to avoid the acknowledgment. But when Mrs. Gresham, who sat beside him, put some leading questions as to their farther movements, he took refuge in a blank un- certainty. They were tied by nothing, he remarked, and might go where the fancy took them. He spoke as if he were a man to

whom decision was a labour, and who was
moved by any passing influence, and he even
announced boldly that it was a great mistake
to be bound by plans when you were only
two in number.   A larger party, he said, was
a different matter, for then it was necessary
to secure accommodation a day or two
beforehand.

'Well,' said Mrs. Gresham helplessly, 'I
don't think it can very well be worse than
this; and Mr. Gresham telegraphed directly
he knew you were coming, so that he would·
have someone to speak to.'

Lancaster gazed at her.

'You knew we were coming?' he said
blankly.

'Yes, of course,' said the lady; 'only, after
what you have just said, I wonder you knew
yourself.'

'But who could have told you?'

'Mr. Gresham, who told you that Sir Henry
Lancaster was coming here?'

'Mark,' answered that gentleman concisely, signifying across the table that his son was the person to whom he alluded.

The Lancasters were at the top of the table, and the Gresham family having divided, half were on one side and half on the other. Next to Lady Lancaster came the daughter, and beyond the daughter the son. Joan at this moment leaned forward across her husband and spoke hurriedly to Mrs. Gresham.

'Weren't you frightened at those very steep zigzags as we came up?' she said. 'I thought them quite dreadful, only the horses seemed to be able to climb like cats, and we had such a good driver!'

'I don't know, I'm sure, whether he was good or not,' said Mrs. Gresham. 'I presume Mr. Gresham got the best that was to be had, but I didn't look. I kept my eyes fast most of the way. It's a tempting of Providence, and I suppose one day we shall suffer for it; but if it's got to be done, I'll do it.'

'I didn't know that you were frightened,' said Lancaster in a low voice to his wife.

'I leave it to Mark,' said Mr. Gresham. 'I'd sooner be at home any day.'

'Oh, I thought it beautiful!' exclaimed his daughter, anxious to repair the family taste. 'I am sure you must have admired it greatly, Lady Lancaster. I don't know what I thought the most beautiful. Those lovely mountains!—and then I liked the little streams so much, and the nice brown houses, and the flowers! I hope—don't you?—that we shall be able to pick quantities of flowers to-morrow.'   .

'Well, you may walk as much as you please, Floss, as long as I haven't to get out of the carriage,' remarked her mother.

'Then you are going on?' inquired Lancaster, in tones of studied calm.

'We're not going to stay here, I imagine,' returned Mrs. Gresham, staring.

'We're going up the mountain,' said her son.

' In that case, I am afraid you say good-bye to your carriage,' Lancaster hinted.

Mrs. Gresham looked at her husband.

' I presume you've made some arrangements, Mr. Gresham ? I don't walk, and I don't ride, and that I wished to be understood from the first.'

' I leave it to Mark. He makes the arrangements, and I pay,' that gentleman returned.

' Of course you can't drive a carriage up a mountain,' the young man muttered impatiently.

' Well, I don't walk and I don't ride,' repeated his mother.

' There is an excellent carriage-road to the Rhone Glacier,' remarked her neighbour insinuatingly.

' Oh no, we must go up the mountain. I am certain it must be quite, quite beautiful,' cried Florence. ' Mamma will make up her mind to it when she sees how easy it is.'

' If it's got to be done, I'll do it,' returned Mrs. Gresham ; ' but I don't walk and I don't ride.'

' Isn't there something ? I think it is a *chaise à porteur,*' suggested Joan, in a low voice.

' Oh, to be sure, of course !' cried the young man rather loudly. ' Some of us might have thought of that before. My mother is most awfully obliged to you, Lady Lancaster, for suggesting it.   It's the very thing.'

' But how could you—how could you, Joan !' remonstrated her husband afterwards, when he had drawn her out and through the village, and they were walking through a flowery meadow and by the side of the foaming mountain stream which dashed gaily over its stones.   There were delicate lights in the sky, a pale, tender dusk creeping over the little village, with its fir-trees and its belfried church ; herds of goats were trooping home, and everything was very peaceful and still under the shadow of the great mountain. 'It was all going as nicely as possible. If you hadn't offered a helping hand, to-morrow would have seen us free of them.'

'It would have been too cruel, wouldn't it?' said Joan, smiling at him. 'I thought the poor thing was so heroic, shutting her eyes and coming up those zigzags, that I was obliged just to whisper the word *chaise à porteur*. It's a great big mountain. Isn't there room for all of us?'

'You're better than I am,' said Lancaster, looking at her fondly. 'I'll learn to be less savage. And, after all, as you say, we needn't be always knocking up against them.'

'We needn't stay, if that's all,' she said carelessly.

'Oh, as to that,' he returned, 'I suspect they'll go first. It'll take a good deal to get me off. This is the spot I've been longing for ever since we started. This is one of the places I told you about—on the line and yet

off it.   People come here, of course, but
generally they are not people of the Gresham
type, but those who really care for what they
find.   One has to put up with those big
overgrown hotels, and you can see now for
yourself what a refreshment there is in these
mountain places—at any rate, you will see,
when we get up to-morrow.'

He was in such spirits himself that he did
not notice her want of enthusiasm.   She
looked round her and shivered slightly.   Was
this world, this world of solitude, what she
had looked forward to when she married?
Was she to be condemned to periodical in-
flictions of dulness such as this?   Why,
this—this was no better than Ashbury; it
even struck her as more lonely.   What she
wished for was society, people, companionship.   How glad she was that the Greshams
were going up, since even the Greshams were
better than nobody; and, indeed, she did not
find Mr. Mark Gresham's rather too openly

expressed admiration at all disagreeable. She was very glad that she had contrived to let drop before him the name of their destination, and she reflected that, in spite of her husband, he should know where they were going next. She made an excuse of fatigue, and went back to the inn, and, finding young Gresham and his sister outside the door, sat down there, and begged Lancaster to go and smoke his cigar. When he returned, it momentarily jarred upon him to hear her laughing more merrily than she had laughed for the day; but she called him to her with the prettiest grace in the world, and he put down her willingness to be amused to her sweetness and kindly temper.

The next morning they went up to the little hotel half-way up the mountain, Joan riding. Lancaster was like a boy in his enjoyment of the air, the flowers, the beauty. He had Joan all to himself. He had dismissed from his mind all care. What could come to trouble him? The fine aromatic air blowing off the fir-trees, the exhilarating peeps of snow, the presence of the girl he loved and had won, gave him an almost intoxicating lightness of spirit, and he was sorry when the scrambling walk was over, and there lay the little hotel on its plateau. But Joan looked with dismay at its minute solitariness, for it seemed small enough in the midst of its surroundings.

'Where are the people?' she asked anxiously.

'There's the landlord at the door. I don't expect there will be many others to be seen just now, for some are sure to have gone up the mountain, and we met a good many coming down.'

Well—he had his way. He took his wife for a rambling walk, and what was wanting? The early beauty of the flowers was over, but they were there still in abundance, and the air was scented with them. Down below

them mists drifted over little hamlets, each
with its graceful bell-tower. Nothing could
have been more delightful than the spring of
the short turf, the vigorous growth of the
brief strong summer. The beautiful little
dun cattle on the high pastures lifted their
heads and looked impatiently at the intruders.
It was just as Lancaster had pictured when
he dreamed of the dear delight of seeing her
joy in it all, and it was all there, except—
was it the joy? Something — some cold
cloud, as light and intangible as the vapour
drifting over the hills—seemed suddenly to
wrap him round, and chill him to the heart.
It was intangible. He could not take hold
of it—he could not beat it away ; but it was
cold as death. It could not be traced to
words or looks, yet it touched them all.
It was not substantial enough for a name
—it could not be called indifference, or
temper, or opposition ; yet it was enough
to take the light and colour out of what

was before him, and, while it lasted, to numb him with its chill. He felt suddenly as if she did not love him.

The sensation passed. Looking back, indeed, he could hardly say how it had come.

As they made their way back to the hotel, Joan's spirits seemed to revive; and she walked more briskly, taking more sympathetic notice of the things about her. And though she had said that she was tired and should lie down, when she reached the house she had apparently forgotten her fatigue.

' The Greshams have come !' she exclaimed eagerly. ' Oh, I must find out how that *chaise à porteur* succeeded. I see them strolling over there, and looking so unhappy ! Will you come, or must you write your letters ?'

' I must write,' said her husband. ' Do you really care to join them ?'

' Oh yes !' she said with alacrity.

And as she hurried off she turned to kiss her hand.

He stood watching her, a strange sinking at his heart.

There was something he could not understand — a contradiction of his preconceived ideas troubling him; and yet, as he turned to go upstairs, he told himself that he was a fool to take such trifles to heart. They had been nothing after all—nothing, at least, but the pettiest indications. He tried to fling off the fanciful burden; he told himself that he was unjust to Joan; but he could not succeed in getting rid of the impression. Angry with himself and with this cold blast of doubt, he sat down to his writing, and flung himself into business, which but that morning he had decided might wait his leisure, succeeding for a time in baffling the enemy by giving all his mind to the matters in hand. He finished his letters; the cloud had once more floated off, and when he stood

up it was with a laugh at his own folly. The
laugh was lightly echoed outside, and from
his window he saw Joan scrambling down
a little gully near the house with Mr. Mark
Gresham and his sister. They were talking
gaily together, and, as she saw him, she
waved her hand. He waved back again.
Not another misgiving would he allow
himself. Was it not only another proof of
her sweet wholesome nature that she should
find something beyond the inanity and pomp
of riches, where he could see these only ?
And as for that other, that far more dis-
tracting thought, could he expect her to
love him as he loved her—as yet ? Should
he not be well content with the affection
she gave him, and more than content to
feel that now he might set himself to win
the deeper love ?

Later in the afternoon a party came down
from the mountain, the ladies very hot and
sunburnt, but all enthusiastic. They had

gone up in three hours; they had come down in one. The Matterhorn and Monte Rosa group were hazy, but the Jungfrau, Mönch, Eiger, Finsterhorn, Oberaarhorn, Monte Leone, were magnificently seen, and they were loud in their praises of the deep indigo colour of the little Marjelen See.

'We will go up to-morrow, Joan,' said her husband cheerfully.

'When?'

'Early. Then we shall get all the beauty of the morning.'

'Oh, not too early! They say other people will come up from Viesch in the morning, and then we might be a good party.'

'As you like,' he said briefly.

Joan made a centre of liveliness that evening; he felt rather out of it, but she was her radiant self again, and he tried to think that it was all very pleasant. They had unearthed some old racing game from a corner of the little salon, and as nobody quite knew how it was played, there were plenty of suggestions and a good deal of laughter. What annoyed Lancaster was the kind of easy familiarity which Mr. Mark Gresham affected; he rather fixed his thoughts upon this because annoyance was better than the ache which came in spite of his will when he saw Joan smiling upon these strange men with the same smile which he had liked to feel was all his own. He was sitting sideways on his chair, apparently reading a newspaper, but he really saw her all the while. Mrs. Gresham every now and then threw in a remark, from which it appeared that she took him to be a much older man than he was.

'Pleasant to see the young people enjoying themselves, isn't it?' she said. 'There's Mark: I will say he's a host in himself on an evening like this, for there's a something about him which sets everybody at their ease at once. Mr. Gresham gets cross sometimes because Mark doesn't work so well as he might, but I say, " Never mind, father; he's one always to make his way." And so he is.'

' Really ?' remarked Lancaster, in an unpromising voice.

' Yes, indeed. He's like Lady Lancaster in liveliness. What a pretty young creature she is! Floss has quite lost her heart to her. I tell Floss she's too romantic ; but when once she takes a fancy she's so devoted. You'll all go up the mountain to-morrow, I presume ? and I'll ask you, Sir Henry, to keep an eye on Floss, and not let her overdo it. When she's excited she gets so rash. Her feelings run away with her, that's what they do !'

' Hadn't you better go yourself ?' asked Lancaster.

Mrs. Gresham, however, protested that if he were of the party she should have no fear, and Lancaster perceived that by the irony of fate he was to be elected as Miss Gresham's guardian.

The next morning he thought himself lucky to get his wife out of the house by herself, though it was for no more than a little stroll to see the indescribable beauty of the Weisshorn, standing up against a pale and silvery sky. When they came back, and he spoke about a guide for their own climb, the landlord shook his head and doubted the weather holding out; and, indeed, it was soon evident that clouds were rapidly sweeping up, and a few distant mutterings gave warning of the coming of the storm. The people who had already accomplished their ascent had started early for the Bel Alp, and only one man, elderly and red-faced, had come up from the valley. By-and-by the rain began, and though at first it was hoped it might be no more than a short and sharp thunderstorm, it continued steadily, and there was no possibility of attempting the moun-

tain. Joan was very disconsolate. The
Greshams were better than no one, but they
did not count for much, and she hated the
little hotel, the absence of society, and the
feeling of being in the heart of a cloud. She
came to her husband disconsolately.

'Oh, Henry, they say it sometimes goes
on like this for days.'

'But you don't believe them?'

'Yes, I do. And just consider. Even if
to-morrow is fine, the day after may be
wet.'

'Well, O logician, shall we not have
achieved our object by that time? Shall we
not have gone up?'

'Yes. But if the next day is wet, we
shan't be able to get away.'

She came close to him as she spoke, and
laid her head upon his shoulder, lifting her
lovely eyes to his. But in spite of their
charm he felt a pang.

'You don't like it? You want to go?'

'Oh, it's lovely, but it's a little dreary. Nobody but the Greshams!'

She made a laughing face.

'Oh, the Greshams! Certainly I don't want to see the Greshams again!' cried Lancaster hastily.

'There, then! If we stay here, we shall be always knocking up against them,' said Joan, with triumph.

'You wish to go?'

'Who would care to stay?' she returned more petulantly.

They went. How could he refuse her? And though it hurt him to think that she did not care for even so much solitude shared with him, he found a pleasure in bringing his own strong will into subjection for her dear sake. The next day was fine, and instead of going up the mountain they set their faces down. Mark Gresham proposed the others leaving at the same time, but Lancaster said coolly that they had made their own arrangements.

'I hope we have done with them,' he remarked, as he and Joan went swinging down
the steep path. As she did not answer, he
added : 'That young fellow struck me last
evening as decidedly objectionable.'

'Did you think so?' she said lightly.
'Well, they're left behind now.'

He laughed happily.

'Yes. They won't track us this time so
easily.'

Joan was in spirits. They picked up the
maid and drove to the Rhone Glacier, and
the next day over the Furka to Andermatt.
There they spent Sunday, and the following
morning very early crossed the cold and
dreary Oberalp down to flowery Dis-
sentis.

'By the way, Joan,' said her husband,
laughing, 'I forgot until this moment that
last night I had a panic. I could have vowed
that I heard Mrs. Gresham's voice in the
passage. But it is most unlikely.'

He was not looking at her, and did not see the colour spring into her face.

'Oh, very unlikely!' she said hurriedly.

At Trons, with a change of drivers, began a series of misadventures. He nearly drove into a torrent, and he managed to smash the pole in turning into a covered bridge across the Rhine. Lancaster determined to get rid of the fellow at Ilanz. Meanwhile, for the coming descent he insisted upon the third horse being taken off. The remaining two were chestnuts, and one seemed to him an ill-tempered brute. The steep zigzags were more than usually unprotected. At the bottom of the precipitous bank flowed the Rhine. Suddenly the off-horse shied violently. The next moment the fore-wheel was over the edge; the carriage hung, as it were, upon destruction. Lancaster caught Joan to him, sprang out, and rushed to the horses' heads, shouting to the maid and the driver. But by this time the carriage was too far gone to be

recovered. The struggling horses were plung-
ing and kicking. The maid leapt off, and in
another instant there was an awful crash, and
carriage, horses, and men were over the
precipice.

CHAPTER XXI.

So quickly had the accident happened, so bewildered was Joan by the shock and the fall, that for one instant, as she regained her feet and the carriage crashed over, she did not realize what had happened. The next moment the dreadful silence, succeeding a sickening cry, the dreadful vacuum where before had been a struggling mass, forced the horrible reality upon her, and with another cry, almost as despairing as that which had but just died away, she dragged herself to the broken edge and leaned over.

Below her, at no great distance, she saw

her husband painfully putting himself into a
safer position by the help of a slender bush,
so slender and frail that it threatened at each
tug to give way. As the terrified horses
were drawn over the edge by the falling
carriage, he had let go his hold, and although
not in time to save himself from going over
with them, he fell a little on one side of the
track caused by their descent, and without
the impetus received by the unlucky driver,
who, momentarily delayed by the maid, only
sprang off at the instant of the fall. Lancaster
was mercifully checked for a second by this
little group of bushes, almost the only ones
which for some distance broke the bare precipitous bank. He clutched at them, dug in
his heels, and was saved so far that he was,
at any rate, arrested. His position, for so
heavy a man, was, however, still precarious,
and when Joan's rapturous call reached him,
he scarcely dared to answer her. Her wits,
however, came quickly back. She looked

hastily around. No one was near. The maid still lay on the ground, more frightened than hurt, but that she could not know. Some men on the opposite side of the river, down below, were running and shouting, having seen the accident, but they were too far away to give the immediate help she wanted. Rope — that was the thing, the necessary thing—how could she get it ? Then in a moment she had snatched off a long black lace scarf twisted round her neck, and flung one end over the edge. At intervals along the zigzag there were set short upright stones to mark the road ; one of these was fortunately at this spot, and Joan, kneeling down behind it, clutched the end of the scarf with the strength of desperation. Happily she was strong, for at times the strain on her wrists and arms seemed as if it might tear them out of their sockets ; but she held on bravely, and Lancaster, having all his wits about him, moved warily, testing the loose

rubble before he tried it, and presently was
able to pass his arm round the stone, and hoist
himself to her side. As he did so, with the
reaction and the strain, Joan's strength failed,
and she fell back fainting. The maid, who
had been gradually coming round to a sense
of what had happened, raised herself on her
elbow and began to scream. Lancaster told
her savagely to be quiet ; he was breath-
ing heavily as he bent over his young
wife, and passionately imploring her to
look up.

' I am safe, Joan—I am safe !' he cried.

She opened her eyes presently, closed
them, opened them again, and sat up with
a shudder. Her husband's arms were
around her, and he was kissing her with
violence.

' You are not hurt ?' he demanded.

She pushed back the hair from her fore-
head.

' I thought we were falling,' she said in a

terrified voice. 'What has happened?' and then, in an agony, 'Help, help!'

'Don't look,' he said tenderly; 'both of us are safe—and Butler.   Let me lift you across the road to her.'

He tried to raise her as he spoke, but his face turned an ashen white, and he put her gently down again.

'Can you manage to walk with my arm round you?   There!   Wait here till I come back.'

But she clung to him.

'Where are you going?   Don't go!   Oh, the poor man and the horses!'

'He may have been saved as I was. Don't stop me, my dearest; I must do what I can.'

'You can't go down that—that awful place!   And I saw men, I did indeed!   They were running!   Henry!'

He disengaged himself from her clinging arms.

'Don't stop me, Joan,' he repeated. He walked to the edge and looked over. Down below, and partly in the river, lay a great inert mass ; carriage and horses were there all tumbled together and without movement. He secretly thought that the poor driver was there, too. He shouted, and there was certainly an answer, but it appeared to come from higher up the river. The next moment he felt Joan's clasp on his arm. She was deadly pale, but she had got back her self-possession, and though her voice trembled, she spoke without excitement.

'You must try the road ; you see that it is impossible for you to go down the face of this precipice.'

'It should not be impossible,' he said slowly, 'but I believe I can't do it. Yes, I must find an easier way. Promise me to stay with Butler.'

'Very well.'

He went quickly away, not daring to look back at her, and, in spite of giddiness, she stood watching the dreadful heap below, uncertain whether what she now and then noticed was really movement, or only the swirl of the passing current. It seemed ages to her, but Lancaster had not really been gone many minutes before she saw that other help was at hand—that the three or four men she had noticed had crossed the river at some point higher up, and were now running along below her. She watched them reach the dark mass, pause, prod it with a pole, hang about it, then two or three of them disengaged themselves and ran on where a little projection concealed them from sight. A sickening sensation seized her; she pressed her hands on her eyes and moved back to the maid, who was weeping and declaring that such a fright would be her death, but who had really only received a few bruises. Joan tried to comfort her, and presently saw her husband coming slowly up the hill. She ran to him, and he put his arm round her.

' I couldn't do it,' he said, in rather a dull voice ; ' I believe I have strained my back or something. And there are men down there.'

' Yes, I know,' she returned. ' Oh, I am glad you did not try! Sit down ; sit down on that bank and rest.'

He did as she told him. It was sweet to him to be cared for by her ; there was such an intoxication in it that for the moment he forgot everything else.

' Turn your head so that I may see you, Joan,' he said persuasively.

She turned to him, and, in spite of her pallor, he thought she had never looked so beautiful. For a few minutes he was silent; then he said :

' We had better walk down the zigzags, if you feel strong enough. The men will know, from only seeing two horses, in which direction we were going, and further on they will be able to get up to the road.'

' But—can you walk ?'

31—2

'Yes,' he returned briefly.

They started therefore—the maid, still tearful, following.

'The first châlet we reach we will stop at, and send on to Ilanz for some sort of carriage,' went on Lancaster.

'Henry,' began the girl fearfully, 'is there any hope, do you think?'

'A little. Having scrambled out of it myself, I don't despair.'

'But the poor horses?'

Lancaster shook his head.

'Poor beasts! No; I only hope it was soon over. Don't talk of it—don't think of it. Are you sure you are all right?'

They went on; the zigzags seemed endless; no house appeared in sight. They could see that more men gathered below, and one detached himself, or was sent off, apparently with the intention of reaching the travellers. Joan walked quickly on; now that help was there she could not bear to look towards that dreadful spot. Presently Lancaster broke the silence.

' Here comes another question,' he said.

' What ?'

' A storm will be upon us in a few minutes, and how are you both to be sheltered ?'

With her mind full of other thoughts, Joan had not noticed the threatening cloud that was sweeping up across the brilliant blue and white of the sky. A wind had arisen, and was momentarily increasing in power, rushing along the valley, and beating the river into foam. Lancaster looked anxiously at his wife as he spoke.

' Never mind,' said Joan bravely. ' What does such a little thing matter ? If we walk quicker we must come to some châlet or tree before long.'

But it seemed as if Lancaster were not willing to walk quicker. He sent the maid on, however, and he and Joan followed. A

few heavy drops fell with soft thuds on the
hard ground, and the maid, who was soon
well in front, turned round and made signs
that something was in sight, just as a peal of
thunder rumbled along the mountains.

'Go on, Joan,' said her husband, releasing
her. 'Run, if you can.'

'I am afraid you are more hurt than you
will allow?' she questioned.

'You should rather be surprised to see
me marching down the hill at all,' he returned, smiling. 'I don't fall like a feather,
and I'm wonderfully lucky to have got off
with a little strain. Run!'

What had been seen turned out to be a
load of timber flung down by the side of
the road. As a low wall had been raised,
it is probable that it was intended to build
a châlet on the spot; but meanwhile the
timbers on the lee side made a fairly effective
protection against the driving storm, and
there Joan and the maid crouched, while Sir

Henry kept on the look-out, anxious not to lose the messenger from below. But before he came, and while the rain was lashing down in sheets, a welcome sound reached their ears—the rumble of wheels—and in a few minutes' time a large travelling carriage came trundling down the zigzags. The hood was up, and its occupants were well hidden by this, and by dripping umbrellas, so that they would have passed the little group without notice if Lancaster had not stepped forward and signed to the driver to stop. The next moment he had an impulse of regret, for the heads which immediately appeared were those of the Greshams.

There was an instant outcry, a chorus of 'Oh's!' questions which left no room for answers, exclamations, wonderment, offers of assistance. Their carriage had been upset? Oh, dreadful! Where was it? How was it they had not seen it? How lucky that they had come by! Was dear

Lady Lancaster *quite* unhurt? And Sir Henry? And the maid? Now she must get in, he must get in, they all must get in. Sir Henry, who felt that his first impulse had been ungrateful, accepted the offer for his wife.

'If you will kindly take her as far as Ilanz,' he said, 'she will be able to send back a carriage for us.'

At this they exclaimed.

'We can't leave you here in the middle of the road. I presume that Mark can walk,' said Mrs. Gresham, 'and the maid go with the driver. Just you get in, Lady Lancaster, and you'll see that Sir Henry will be able to squeeze in, though I can't say it's much of a vehicle.'

'It's the biggest there was,' said her husband defensively.

'You are very good,' said Lancaster, 'but it is necessary for me to wait here and see about the—carriage.'

' Why, where *is* the carriage ?' asked young Gresham, staring round.

Lancaster ignored the question, and went on :

' It will be kind of you to take my wife and the maid, if you can really manage it without inconvenience, and if Mr. Gresham does not mind waiting ?'

' Oh, if you won't come, Mark may as well,' returned Mark's mother. ' There's plenty of room for Floss between me and you, Lady Lancaster, where it's dry, and the gentlemen can sit opposite. I don't hold with walking.'

So it was settled, and Joan, for reasons of her own, was really thankful that the young man did not stay with her husband. She leaned forward, heedless of the heavy rain, smiling and waving, as the carriage drove off, and Sir Henry went back to his shelter. In spite of all that had happened, he carried a lighter heart than he had known for days. Joan had been drawn nearer to him. This

Joan, helpful, brave, kind, had been the Joan
he had imagined, not the Joan whose indifference had wounded him so lately.   It was joy
to feel that he had been unjust.   He smote
himself thankfully with sharpest reproaches.
He had had no right to demand such heaped-
up measure from her.   He should be more
patient, less exacting—so long as he could
pour all this blame upon himself it was very
well with him, and for a little while he forgot
the tragedy he was waiting to hear, the fast-
sweeping storm, and the pain in his back.
In about five minutes' time these were re-
called to him by the appearance of the messenger from below—a young lad so greatly
excited by his errand that Lancaster had
some difficulty in interpreting his speech.
He made out at last, to his great relief, that
the driver was not killed.   They believed his
leg was broken, but they had sent for a man
who had great local fame as a bone-setter,
and would not bring him on until he had seen

him. As for the carriage and the horses, the young man's pantomime was sufficiently expressive. Boxes were burst; a good deal had been swept away by the river. Meanwhile, the boy brought with him a bundle of wraps and umbrellas, with not so much as a stick injured, and a black leather bag of greater value to its owner. He was so curious to know what had happened that he asked more questions than Lancaster, but at last he was dismissed with instructions to bring all that could be saved to Ilanz.

The storm was over. The lashing rain slackened, came down again heavier than ever, and gradually ceased. Out of the mist stole the forms of the mountains, and the colours which had been hidden under a gray pall were now more fresh and vivid than before. A delicious fragrance filled the cool air. The sun turned everything into sparkling, flashing beauty, even the little rain-rivers running down the road. Lancaster came out of his shelter and walked down the zigzags slowly, because of the pain in his back. He thought that in his fall he must have struck it either against a stone or across the stem of the bushes which had saved his life, and then perhaps got a strain in the attempt to climb the bank. But he imagined that a little care would soon cure it. However, he could as yet only walk slowly and with difficulty, so that it seemed a long while before he saw a small carriage crawling up towards him.

He was aware of a quite unreasonable pang when he saw that it was empty. How could he have expected Joan, shaken and terrified as she had been, to come back for him ? He did not expect it—he would have been vexed if she had been so imprudent, and yet—there was that momentary pang. To have seen her looking out, watching for him, would have been so sweet ! To have supposed that she was a little anxious, even if it had been foolishly anxious, about his

hurt, would have been such delicious foolishness !

But she was not there, and he took himself
soundly to task for his selfishness.

It was better, a hundred times better, that
she should be sensibly resting at the inn.   No
doubt the Greshams had gone on ; and then
he began to reflect, with a half-laugh, upon
the absurdity of the fate which, in spite of all
their efforts to keep their own proceedings
wrapped in mystery, sent the Greshams per-
sistently in their track.   There were so many
points where they might have been expected
to diverge.   There was the Rhone Glacier,
and after that Andermatt.   Surely, it would
only have been reasonable of them to turn off
from Andermatt either to Lucerne or by the
St. Gothard into Italy. Why on earth must they
stick to their heels ?   He could not even feel
very grateful to them for their opportune over-
taking on that afternoon.   Any other carriage
would have been welcome, but gratitude due

to the Greshams seemed to open out vistas of heavy service. Mrs. Gresham was the best of the lot : her husband creaked of money ; the son struck him as under-bred and the daughter as affected. Affectation was so unendurable to Lancaster, that where it existed he was hardly just.

However, as he drove on, these thoughts, of which he was in truth secretly ashamed, were forced out of his head by the exceeding beauty of things about him. He found himself crawling up a hill towards Ilanz, which lay amid cherry and walnut trees—a picturesque heaped-up mass of châlet and church, crowned by the tall tower of a castle. Down below, the Rhine pierced its way through the long narrow valley ; precipitous crags shot upwards on its other side, and above and beyond lay mountains and one softly-rounded head of snow. Gleams of sunshine shot out here and there from behind the great white clouds, which, rent by the storm, were ominously gathering again ; and as he looked, one brilliant ray struck the little tower on the hill-crest, and brought out every detail with startling clearness.

At the door of the little inn stood the Greshams' carriage, and as soon as his own rattled up, Joan came flying out to meet him and to hear his news.

' You poor fellow,' she cried pitifully ; ' how tired you must have been of waiting ! Come in, come in ! We told them to keep something hot for you, and you will just have time to eat it before we start.'

' Start ? Have you got a carriage, then, and settled everything, you clever young woman ?'

' Oh, well, carriage—there's no other carriage than this.'

' This shanderydan !'

' It is very shaky, isn't it ?' said Joan eagerly.

' Rather ! However, we must make the

best of it.   I suppose it will keep the rain off.
But it's a confounded nuisance.'

'Mrs. Gresham is very kind—she wants
me to go on with them,'—hesitatingly.

'You'd prefer the shanderydan, I presume,'
said Lancaster, laughing.   'What makes her
" presume " so much ?'

'I think you are hard on them,' said Joan,
drawing herself away a little.   'I think they
are very good-natured.'

'Good-natured ?   Good heavens, to be sure
they are !   Only too good-natured !   Yes, and
you're right, Joan ; they got us out of a
hobble to-day, and one oughtn't to laugh at
them.   I'll go and say all that's proper.'

'But,' detaining him, 'I really think that
—one of us had better go with them.'

'One of us ?'   Lancaster laughed ; but the
next moment his laugh ended.   'One of us ?
That could only be you.'

'I shouldn't mind,' she said quickly, and
without looking up.   'I think Mr. Gresham

could stay and share this thing, and then we should all be quite comfortable and have plenty of room. Aren't you glad about the poor driver? And isn't it wonderful, quite wonderful, that he should have fallen all that way and not been killed?' Seeing that he did not answer, she went on: 'We could all start together, you know, and change companions occasionally. Their carriage is ordered in half an hour, and there is some food all ready for you.'

'I cannot start in half an hour,' said Sir Henry gravely. 'I must see about the man—'

'You could leave money for him.'

'And look after our things. You forget that all we have has to be fished out of the Rhine.'

Her face fell.

'It is such a miserable little place!' she exclaimed disconsolately. 'And, really, if you must stay, I can't see of what possible use I should be.'

'You mean,' he said, after a momentary blank pause, 'that you would prefer to go on with these people?'

'Yes, of course I do,' she said, quickly and brightly. 'All this has been so horrid that I shall always hate the name of this place, and the sooner I can turn my back upon it the better I shall be pleased. Then I could have everything ready at Coire, and telegraph for some clothes. It would be a good thing to telegraph, wouldn't it?'

Alas for his dream!

Words, looks, all spoke too unmistakably. They had only been married one short fortnight, and already the companionship, which to him had seemed so enchanting, was grown so wearisome to her that she even preferred the society of these second-rate, commonplace people. He had, indeed, suffered misgivings in the last few days that this might be so, but he had chased them from him; he had reproached himself for having allowed them to invade his heart—had owned that he might have magnified trifles. But, to-day —to-day, when they had escaped a common peril; when he, at any rate, had been saved from the very jaws of a frightful danger— he had felt as if even the separation of the past hour would have been as unendurable to her as to him. He could not bear to let her out of his sight, and he had expected, never doubted, to find the same thrill of love in her. And now, she was looking at him, clinging to his arm, it was true; but looks and touch seemed to stab rather than comfort, and drove a haunting fear into his mind.

All that he said, however, was that she must do what she liked best, and if she read any disappointment in his tones, she did not let it affect her purpose. At this moment, indeed, the Greshams came out into the little passage, insufferably familiar and sympathetic, as Lancaster felt, and felt, even then, with self-reproach. He had all his

life mocked at the sharp distinctions which
society draws—it had pleased him to make
scathing remarks as to its sensitiveness; and
here he was conscious of his own repugnance
to accept a favour at the hands of people
who, so far as he knew, had no other sin
than that of the want of some society virtues.
Yet he—he, the mocker, the leveller—here
was he become suddenly fastidiously critical
—aware of Mr. Gresham's pompous vul-
garity, of Mrs. Gresham's too familiar bene-
volence, of the daughter's self-conscious-
ness, of the son's uneasy attempt at ease.
Could Joan really like their company, or was
it no more than that kindness of heart with
which he credited her? The twist in his
mouth became more acute as he watched
her. This was not toleration, not mere
good-nature; she smiled, brightened, dimpled,
chatted with evident pleasure, and appeared
to be on the best of terms with both Mr.
Mark Gresham and his sister. And though

Sir Henry had never actually consented to the plan by which she was to precede him to Coire, Joan acted as if there were no question of her not doing so, and, moreover, was evidently in a hurry to start.

Inwardly, Lancaster fumed, but he said no more, except to reject shortly Mr. Gresham's offer to remain and share his carriage. He made it very plain that this would not be at all acceptable. His wife he could not, or would not, influence, but he told himself that at least he would not submit to the companionship of this tiresome old man. So Joan drove away, smiling and waving her hand, and Mrs. Gresham called out that he needn't be afraid—they would take excellent care of her. Lancaster looked and listened in a sort of fury. He was not naturally a very patient man, though he had an immense amount of self-control. He felt now as if he had suffered a moral collapse. If his wife had not married him for love, for what had she married him ? She needed neither money nor position.

There was a good deal to be done, and he did it. The unfortunate driver, bruised, shaken, and with a broken leg, was established in a châlet with a nurse. Most of the boxes were fished out of the Rhine : some of the contents were hopelessly spoiled ; others, after drying, were little the worse ; and Butler found a very exciting operation in superintending all this sorting and re-packing; but as it became evident that it was growing too late to drive on to Coire, Lancaster became the more restless. With a rush of relenting tenderness, he tried to persuade himself that Joan would be uneasy, would sit up, listening and longing, and finally decreed that while the wrecked boxes should follow the next morning, he would himself push on that night to Coire. As he could not get a carriage beyond Reichenau, he walked the rest of the way.

CHAPTER XXII.

WHEN a man's whole nature has been shaken, there is nothing so healing and restoring as a walk under the stars. The smaller frets of life, which have more to do with the greater than we are ready to admit, fall away and shrivel into nothingness; all his outlines gain in breadth, and he judges with larger charity. As Lancaster strode along, with the dim shapes of the silent hills lifting themselves towards the skies, and with no sound except the quick gurgle of a little mountain stream, or the tinkle of a cow-bell, to break the stillness, his misgivings passed away like mists swept out of the valley.

Once more he declared to himself that he had been unjust to his young wife, once more vowed that only his own impatience was to blame. He was glad that he had resolved to push on to Coire, though he began to feel tired, in spite of the fresh aromatic air, and to be again conscious of pain where he had struck his back. So indifferent to all but the one overmastering thought had he felt when he was at Ilanz, that he had taken no pains to overcome the driver's reluctance to a late start, and had rather welcomed the strong exercise; but by the time he reached the hotel at Coire he was pretty well worn out, and began to think that he had acted like a fool. He had some difficulty in rousing the porter, and was told that madame had long since retired. He listened at her door, watched by the porter, who regarded him with sleepy suspicion, and, as no sound was audible, gave up his idea of letting her know that he had arrived, and went to his own room, where he spent a bad night, which began with a shivering fit.

In the morning, Joan's greeting was a little constrained. She could be bold when she had others to back her up, but alone her courage rapidly oozed away. Lancaster, however, said not a word of reproach, and she did not allude to—perhaps did not notice—his altered looks. It was Mrs. Gresham who held up her hands when he and his wife appeared in the *salle à manger*.

' Here,' she cried hospitably—' here, we've kept places for you both with us. Come and sit here by me, Sir Henry, and tell me how you got on? You see we took very good care of Lady Lancaster, as I promised. We were a very merry party, weren't we, Floss? I'm sure they made me laugh last night till I ached; I did indeed, Sir Henry. But, I never! you don't look very well! Whatever have you been doing with yourself? Did you get any harm in that nasty accident?'

' A little shake. I shall be all right again in a day or two,' said Sir Henry, trying to speak cordially.

' Well, Lady Lancaster, you'd better look after your husband,' said Mrs. Gresham, full of good-natured concern. ' You'd better see that he doesn't go running up mountains and things, or getting wet, for he isn't fit for it. He doesn't look the same man. I wish there was never anything to do with horses.'

' You must allow me to thank you exceedingly for your very opportune help,' said Sir Henry.

' Help? Oh, you mean picking up Lady Lancaster? Why, that was nothing. Flossy and Mark were as pleased as pleased to have her; and even Mr. Gresham—he never says much—but even he said what a good thing it was that we had come after you.'

Joan, who had looked uneasy, here leaned forward.

' When will Butler be here, Henry?' she

asked hurriedly. 'I want so dreadfully to see
what state my poor things are in after all their
misfortunes. You know I have had to borrow
everything. Do you think I shall find anything to wear?'

'I hope so.'

'You hope, but you don't know. You
don't speak very consolingly. Well, one
thing is certain. We must go straight back
to Paris and shops.'

There was a general cry :

'Oh, dear Lady Lancaster!'

'You don't mean to desert us! By Jove,
that would be awfully hard lines! That
wouldn't be at all fair.'

'Oh no, my dear!' ('My dear!' reflected
the indignant Sir Henry.) 'What should we
do without you? Poor Floss would be quite
lost, and, after we've dragged Mr. Gresham
all this way, you'd never be so unkind. I'm
sure you're as welcome as can be to all my
gowns.'

Lancaster had been as much startled as anyone by this announcement of his young wife. He had longed for the keener air and the fresh beauty of the Engadine heights. But dislike to the Gresham outcry, horror at the idea of their constant companionship, and an unconfessed feeling of illness, made him rapidly turn in his mind the advantages of a change of plan—of going, not to Paris, which he hated, but perhaps to some lesser town, where Joan might repair her wardrobe, and from which they might leisurely branch off to wilder places. He listened silently while the family continued their lamentations, until at last Mr. Mark's repetition of unfairness raised his ire. He leaned forward, and said coolly :

'You are very good to take our departure so much to heart, but may I ask in what the unfairness consists ?'

'Oh, there is no unfairness,' Joan explained quickly again. 'Mr. Gresham was only joking.'

And she whispered something to her neighbour.

'You mustn't mind Mark,' said Mrs. Gresham, comfortably confidential. 'You see, he's a bit disappointed, because he wouldn't let his father rest until he came along just the same way you were coming, and never thought of your changing.'

'Did I ever mention our plans?' asked Sir Henry, with apparent indifference. But the devil of distrust had got hold of him again.

'No, I don't think you did. No; I remember Mr. Gresham saying one day he thought all the better of you because you were pretty close. It was Lady Lancaster, of course, who told Mark, and then, as I said, Mark gave his father no rest, and Flossy was just as bad. Young people do like to be together, don't they, Sir Henry? And when we come out together like this, I generally take their part.'

A great deal more was said, a great many remonstrances were addressed to Joan, but Lancaster did not hear them. When Mrs. Gresham at last made another direct appeal to him, he started.

'I think it probable that we shall turn back, as Lady Lancaster suggests,' he said ; ' but when we have talked it over, no doubt she will let you know.'

And as he spoke he got up from his half-eaten breakfast.

Joan was looking at him fearfully. If she had gone after him and had it out, it might have been far better; but this she did not dare. And if he had spoken, the silent gnawing brooding would have been spared him. As it was, he felt too much dismay, too much shame, at the deception to say a word. The conviction that she did not love him swept back with redoubled force ; but that was a misfortune, a misery—this was more ; this was deceit, this was acting as if she felt active dislike ; and he groaned aloud as he stood in the passage. With all his trust in her thus shaken, the ground reeled. What shipwreck had he made of his life ! Where did he stand ? What was she—this girl whose heart he had flattered himself he could read as an open book ? Why, good heavens ! if he had been so deluded, what security remained ? Lancaster was an honest-hearted, sensible, God-fearing man ; yet at this moment of shock he was as senseless and as full of exaggerated fancies as the veriest fool. Any treatment of his young wife would have been wiser than the stupid plan of saying nothing until she chose to offer some explanation herself.

She avoided him, that was evident, and Lancaster on his part began to dread being alone with her. She waited in the *salle à manger* until she could come out with the Greshams ; then they all fell again upon Sir Henry, imploring him to persuade her to

change her mind. Lancaster muttered something between his teeth; the expression of
his face was not pleasant, as Joan knew from
looking at him when she thought he was not
looking. At last he spoke to her.

'You had better decide finally what you
wish to do.'

'I wish to go to Paris,' she said, trying
to answer lightly.

He went away without another word,
and in the midst of despairing lamentations
Mark Gresham suggested that they should
go out and see the old town.

'I don't suppose Sir Henry will care to
come,' he said significantly.

'Well,' returned his mother, 'I think you'd
better persuade him to keep quiet. He looks
pretty bad; I never saw anyone so changed.'

'I dare say he is shaken,' said Joan;
'and then it was so foolish of him to walk
all those miles! I hope Butler will soon
arrive and set us free.'

She did not feel comfortable, but she allowed the young man to walk by her side, and whisper admiring compliments, which she liked, while conscious that they were not in the best taste. She hurriedly reflected that it was not probable they would ever meet again, and she had grown to look and care for admiration so much that she really craved for it in whatever shape it came. Lancaster did not bestow it as openly as she desired.

Until the time of their own departure she did not see anything of her husband. The Greshams drove away, with many protestations of grief at leaving her behind. Butler and the boxes interested her for awhile, and then they were in the train, and her spirits rose with the thought of Paris.

Lancaster was grave and silent, revolving many things, chiefly their own future. If she did not love him, if she could so readily deceive him, all that he had built upon for that future was roughly overthrown, and all his thoughts of it took a different complexion. It amazed him that she could look as she did, smile as she did ; that what seemed to him so miserable she could treat with indifference. The more he thought of this, the wider the gulf seemed to open between them, and his heart was torn by both anger and grief. Whenever he looked at the beautiful young face grief got the upper hand.

Joan, meanwhile, was well aware that he had been strongly moved by what he had heard ; but when she found that nothing was said, she did not trouble herself much about the matter. His figure did not fill the same place in her thoughts as hers in his ; it rather represented ease, amusement, indulgence, than anything higher or nobler. He was a means to an end. If he were to be cross and disagreeable, she would dislike it—perhaps she would dislike him—very much ; but to any smaller signs of discomposure she was likely to remain indifferent.

Paris was reached in two days. By this time Joan was slightly indignant with her husband ; she missed something which had surrounded her before, and which she liked. She yawned, and looked bored.

Lancaster, meanwhile, who knew nothing of illness, set down some of his physical feelings to the score of worry. He had a vague idea that worry would produce all kinds of discomfort, and he was sufficiently wretched not to be surprised at the result. He could have forgiven her the foolish little deceit, or anything else, if he could have believed that she loved him ; the sting lay in the conviction that she was indifferent. Now he began to long for the old life—the life of hard work, which for awhile he had so gladly pitched on one side ; he said to himself that here, after all, lay his interests, and that by throwing himself into it more keenly than

33—2

ever he could learn to forget—a good deal.
And for this end he was anxious to get back
to England.

But Joan was in no such hurry. She had
never before had unobstructed opportunities
of spending money. The loss of many
things gave her an excuse for replacing them
by others, and her husband made no objection, though Lady Medhurst would have
been shocked at the costly garments which
were put in the place of her carefully-selected
and serviceable clothes. It must be owned
that Joan chose well, and that her taste was
admirable ; but it was thrown away upon Sir
Henry, who did not know what was fashionable or unfashionable, and only longed to see
her in the simple girlish dress which, to him,
had formed part of her charm. Sometimes
he asked himself which was the real Joan
—this or that ; and with the hope of bringing
back past days would watch, and often lavish
a yearning, passionate tenderness upon her.

But it appeared as if now he was too much alive to the real languor of her affection to be content with what had contented him before. Then he had thought that underneath lay, shyly hid, treasures of womanly love, not yet revealed to him; now, it seemed as if all that there was for him—sometimes he believed a little more than really existed —rested on the surface.

So he moodily waited while it pleased Joan to amuse herself in Paris. He did all she asked, went to the theatres, paid her bills, and felt himself outside everything. The life was utterly distasteful to him.

One day, as they were driving down the Champs Elysées, she said suddenly :

' Where are we going next ?'

' Where do you wish to go ?'

She raised her eyebrows.

' Anywhere. I've had enough of Paris.'

He was silent for a moment ; then he said, rather bitterly :

'When you say "anywhere," I presume you have some place in your mind?'

'No, I haven't. I don't want to go to a desert, because I think it's dreadfully dull not to see people. I thought you would have known more here. I am sure there must be heaps of diplomatic men whom you might have found out if you had taken the trouble.'

She said this with such an enchanting smile that he answered hastily :

'We have been only three weeks married!'

'Oh, was that it? Well, now that time is over, I am not going to let you be so unsociable. Tell me about the houses to which we are asked, and I will choose what seems likely to be amusing.'

'I suppose you will go first to Ashbury?'

'To Ashbury!' cried Joan, making a face. 'Henry! why, I have only just come from Ashbury. The idea of supposing that I should want to go back so soon! No, no, no! I must have something newer—something more exciting. We won't have relations, please.'

'We are invited to Denningham.'

Joan was playing with some flowers in her lap. She hesitated.

'Lady Millicent is very nice,' she said slowly ; ' but ——' She stole a smiling glance at him, and shook her head. ' No ; Denningham will not do.'

' Why not ?'

'Why not ? Oh, I don't know. I don't think it would be lively.'

' Is liveliness the only merit in your eyes ?'

' Perhaps,' she said indifferently.

' You should have married someone who more nearly approached your ideal.'

She looked at him with some surprise, but without answering, except by asking :

' Who is there besides ? Old Lady Netley ? She is sure to have someone amusing ; she might do for a few days, and then Penniston.

Penniston is a capital house. Shall I write to-day ? We can just stop in London and see how the house is getting on, and then go north.'

' I have to speak at Leeds on the twenty-ninth.'

' Have you ?' indifferently. ' Well, I dare say you will be able to manage it.'

' Probably,' said Lancaster dryly.

Then his heart reproached him. It was not for this that he should blame her. If he had been mistaken in her character, and had wrongly read her girlish inexperience, his had been the error, and there was nothing for it but patience—patience which with love on either side would have been no hard matter, but without it might be impossible. He was not patient by nature. Enduring he was, and of iron resolve when something lay before him which he had determined to gain ; but simply to suffer was another thing, against which the man's strong will rose in revolt.

Paris was left behind, and in London for a little while Joan was full of the new house and its furniture. She worked untiringly; her energy seemed extraordinary, and her interest in each detail was unfailing. Lancaster had vast arrears of correspondence to make up, so that he had but little time to give her; but though he watched hungrily for a sign that she wanted him, he never had it. People were of course out of town, but one or two who knew him exclaimed at the change in his looks. Joan, however, was too much absorbed in her own pursuits to notice it, and he himself angrily repudiated illness.

One day Lancaster snatched an hour or two and went down to Roehampton; he was surprised when his wife expressed a wish that he had told her, so that she might have gone also.

' You told me you had a hundred things to do,' returned Lancaster.

' I had only one thing, but it was just as

important as a hundred—choosing the draw-ing-room paper. Still, I should have gone with you. I wish you had told me.'

' I imagined you hardly knew them.'

' But I knew your cousin Basil very well, and I like him the best of all your relations. He is so pleasant—the pleasantest man I ever met. Was he there ?'

Lancaster's laugh was hardly agreeable.

' You would not often find him at his home.'

' No, I suppose not. He knows very well how to enjoy himself. Oh dear !' — Joan heaved a sigh ; ' I wish I were a man !'

To this he made no answer. A sort of despair seized him when he thought how often he had condemned the butterfly, idle existence of the women with whom he had been thrown into contact, and here he had taken the same purposeless vanity to his heart. He got up hurriedly and seized a newspaper. But Joan had not done.

' I suppose that Mr. Gray is really very poor ?'

' Very.'

' But can't you, can't someone, do something for him? It seems such a pity that he should not have a chance.'

' He has had plenty of chances.'

Joan laughed.

' You say that so judicially ! I don't think you know the sort of thing he wants. I do. It should be something very brilliant—not quite like other people.'

' Oh, I know exactly, I assure you. I have learned it to my cost.'

' Then try him in it.'

Lancaster looked up quickly.

' What do you mean, Joan ?'

She came and knelt down by his side, laying her head on his arm with a pretty coaxing gesture.

' Oh ! I mean that you must get something nice for poor Mr. Gray, of course. You can. Mr.——' she hesitated; 'somebody told me that you could get anything you chose to ask for.'

'Somebody was a fool, then,' said Lancaster sharply. 'And I'll tell you more, Joan.'

'What?' She had drawn slightly away from him.

'If that idiotic rubbish was correct, which it isn't, I wouldn't lift my finger to get Basil Gray an appointment.'

'Why not?'

'Because he has failed me once.'

He had been going to say something stronger; he changed it to this. She still persisted.

'Oh, he wouldn't fail you again!'

'No,' he said sternly. 'No—he will not.'

'Poor fellow! only think how horrid it must be to be so poor!'

'He is not the one to suffer.'

'Then for the sake of the others—for my sake,' she added, smiling. 'You can't refuse me, when we have been married such a little while.'

He pushed his chair back hastily.

'Do you remember that at last?' he said sharply. Then his voice changed and grew harder. 'Understand once for all, Joan, that I cannot permit you to interfere with matters connected with my office. That is a part of my life with which you have absolutely nothing whatever to do, and with which there must be no meddling.'

Other people had often heard this tone, Joan never. She stared at him and turned a little pale, for until this moment she had imagined her influence to be irresistible, and, knowing how much he loved her, had never supposed that her power could fail. For the first time she felt as if she were feebly beating upon a rock, and the feeling frightened her. And he, who had been chafed by the subject of her asking, was angry with himself the moment he had spoken, and yet—now—did not know what to say to smooth the hardness of his words.

CHAPTER XXIII.

THE great hall at Penniston was the favourite lounging-place of the house. People wrote, read, sang, collected, and had five o'clock tea there; the children raced up and down the broad staircase and round the gallery at the top; the gentlemen made their way to the great log-fire when they came in from shooting. There, buried in a deep arm-chair, Joan was sitting with her young hostess, Lady Selina Selcombe, on the day of their arrival. They had just had tea, and Sir Henry had strolled out to meet the gentlemen. Joan had flung off her long travelling coat, and, in a small plain hat, looked her

freshest and loveliest. Her eyes were sparkling and her voice eager.

' Oh yes,' she was saying, ' it is quite charming to be in England again ! I think it's a
mistake—don't you ?—for people to go and
bury themselves in solitudes. How can one
help being bored ? Henry liked it, and if we
hadn't met with that lucky accident, I suppose
we might have been running up and down
mountains to this day ; but I couldn't go on
with all my things spoiled, could I ? So it
made the most beautiful excuse in the whole
world for coming back again.'

' But Paris—you liked Paris ?'

' I might have liked it—of course I should
have liked it if there had been any fun. But
I have come to the conclusion that in future
I must provide my own fun. Henry hasn't
an idea of that sort of thing ; all his ideas are
much too clever and prosy—you know what
I mean. He has lived in his work, and
fancies when he does take a holiday it must

be just made up of fresh air and fine views
and solitude—solitude! that's the crown of
the whole thing! Isn't it a dreadful fad of
his?'

'You must get him out of that,' said Lady
Selina decidedly.

'Oh yes, I must,' Joan agreed with eagerness. 'That's why I made such a point of
coming here. I knew it would be charming.
I like this hall immensely. What a floor!
Selina '—leaning forward and whispering—
'I know—I am quite certain—that sometimes you dance?'

'Of course we do, my dear. Now that
you are come we'll dance a great deal more—
to-night, if you're not tired.'

'Tired! I'm never tired. Tell me who
you have.'

'The Dunmores—she is a tiresome old
woman, but I had to ask them because of
politics. Their son—not his wife, I'm thankful to say. Elizabeth Ashton—oh, by the

way, she's a cousin of yours, isn't she ? Yes, of course she is. Then there is Lizzy Church, an American girl, and two or three men.'

'Two or three men—but that's so vague. Who are they ? Can they dance ?'

'Now, Joan, don't you think I'm to be trusted ?'

'Yes, yes, of course you are. I know you are. I know everything is certain to be delightful, but still—tell me !'

Lady Selina looked at her with a laugh.

'You care about it all just as much as before you were married, I do believe.'

'Why shouldn't I ?' demanded Joan, throwing up her pretty head. 'I married partly to get it. Oh, Selina, when I look back to those dull dreary days at Ashbury and remember how I just droned through them, and believed all the things papa preached to me about being awkward and not knowing what to say, and really dreaded that charm-

ing, fascinating London life, I can hardly
believe that I could have been such a fool!
Sometimes I did think I was just a little
pretty, but then papa was certain to say
something which took it all out of me
again.'

Lady Selina laughed merrily.

' I wonder you kept your head when you
found out the truth. I wonder '—she had
been going to add—' I wonder that you did
not marry someone with tastes more like
you own,' and she only checked herself just
in time. But Joan guessed something of
her thought.

' I am not quite sure that I didn't lose my
wits a little. I got rather frightened at last
lest I should do something irrevocably foolish.
But marrying Sir Henry was very wise, wasn't
it ? You see, he liked me awfully from the very
first.' Joan tossed her hat on the table, and
leaned back in the great chair, turning her
head with a smile towards her hostess. ' Aw-

fully! And then I heard on all sides that he had never liked anyone before, and I thought it would be such a grand crow over papa—he was always saying that I was so unformed, and that people would laugh at me, and as he had a tremendous respect for Henry I couldn't resist the joke. You never saw anyone so astonished! I was going to have such a scolding, and the scolding just died away in his throat. It *was* fun.'

She laughed at the remembrance, but Lady Selina, who, in spite of all her flightiness, loved her husband, looked doubtful.

'Was that really why you married?' she asked. 'Didn't you care at all for Sir Henry? My dear Joan, I am afraid you must have lost your wits, after all.'

The girl raised her eyebrows.

'Oh, I did care. I really cared for him as much as for anyone else. I thought he was funnily old for his age, and so he is. Oh, Selina, he really is! You should have seen

him in Switzerland. There were some people
there—stupid people, you know, but they were
better than no one—and I encouraged them
to come with us. He didn't like it at all. I
don't know that he's got over it yet. But,
you see, Selina, he must get used to that sort
of thing. Once or twice I've had a panic
lest he should take after papa—think the
only place to live in is the depth of the
country—and I couldn't stand it. I couldn't,
indeed! That was one thing I considered
when I married. I knew he would have to
live in London, because everyone said that
he was an ambitious man, who would like to
get to the top of the tree.'

'Has he changed?'

'I hope not,' said the young wife musingly;
'but I must take care, because once or twice,
as I said, he was inclined to be ridiculous,
and to talk about the charms of living quite
by ourselves. Imagine! I think he begins
to understand that I should hate it. And

now, Selina—you cruel Selina!—you have not told me who you have got here.'

' Captain Brookes.'

' He can dance. Yes, he dances very well.'

' Lord Islington.'

' Oh !' Joan made a dissatisfied face. ' He is so lazy. He is always talking about "such dwedful exertion." '

' My brother Dick.'

' Yes, yes——'

' And Mr. Gray—Mr. Basil Gray.'

As she said this, Lady Selina glanced with some curiosity at Joan. Basil Gray's attentions had been freely discussed, and it had always been supposed that if the matter had only rested with Miss Medhurst, he, and not Sir Henry, would have won the day. If Joan's remarks this afternoon had dispelled the idea, none the less was it possible that she might display some emotion upon hearing that he was in the house. But all that Joan showed was genuine pleasure. She sat upright in the chair and clapped her hands.

'Mr. Gray! Oh, that is capital! He can dance! I don't know anyone who dances like him. Selina, it will be delicious! I was certain I should enjoy myself here, and now, of course, there can be no doubt about it. Only think, if we hadn't had that accident, I might have been kept out in those poky little places, and missed all this! It was horrible at the time, though,' she added reflectively.

'What was it?' asked Lady Selina.

'Henry shall tell you. It's rather odd, but I get a little queer when I talk about it. Don't let us say any more'—jumping up. 'I think I'll go and put myself into a tea-gown, I feel so dusty. I found a particularly nice tea-gown in that corner shop of the Place Vendôme.'

'Things are changed, Joan,' said her hostess, with a laugh.

' I flatter myself they are, my dear. When I think of the frocks I had to wear, and the sort of things Maria used to turn out, I shiver. If we had been poor and obliged to put up with pokiness, I shouldn't have minded one bit ; but all that ugliness to which I was condemned was perfectly unnecessary. Henry has a dreadful inclination that way—at least, he talks about things being simple and girlish, and, of course, I squash such nonsense at once. Now I'm going—I'm gone !' She stopped on the staircase to bend over the balusters and add : ' If you do like the tea-gown, your maid could perfectly well take the pattern, you know.'

' Her head is quite turned,' said Lady Selina afterwards to Elizabeth Ashton.

' It never carried much to keep it steady.'

'Well, I don't know. I never thought Joan a fool. But of all the wives for Sir Henry ! What can have possessed him to marry her ?'

'Oh,' said Elizabeth bitterly, 'the natural inclination of man for the unsuitable.'

'He had better look after her. She has but one idea at present, and that is her own amusement.'

'They will learn to go their separate ways, I suppose.'

'I don't think that will answer for Joan,' Lady Selina returned. 'And I don't know him well enough to be able to guess how he'll act. He strikes me as looking ill. I wonder if he is already *désillusioné*?'

'I don't pity him.'

'Oh, I do. I always pity the men.'

'He had only to open his eyes and see.'

Then the others began to drop into the hall—Mr. Selcombe and two or three others from shooting, and with them Sir Henry, who had walked through the park until he met the party. Lady Selina, who was rather curious as to his sensations, remarked that he flung a quick glance round the hall.

'Joan will be down in a moment,' she explained. 'She has only gone to change her dress.'

As she spoke, Lady Lancaster came slowly down the stairs, stopping on the way to take in the group. Set off by the old oak and the tapestry hangings, her beauty had never looked more radiant, or her dress more perfect.

'By Jove!' ejaculated Mr. Dunmore under his breath.

She kissed Elizabeth, shook hands with Dick Hamerton, Lady Selina's young brother, and began to talk with animation. Lancaster, from a rather shadowy corner, watched her with amazement. Was this the frightened girl who, such a short time ago, had trembled if a stranger so much as addressed her? It was like the transformation of a quiet little English linnet into some brilliant tropical bird. But then—it had been the linnet which had attracted him.

Presently Elizabeth Ashton came across
to him; she, too, had been watching and
wondering.

' Haven't you come home sooner than you
intended?' she asked. ' They wrote from
Ashbury that you meant to stay some time
in Switzerland.'

' It was getting late for the Engadine, and
Joan lost some of her clothes in the Rhine,
which, of course, necessitated a return to
some place where clothes are to be bought.'

The ' of course ' had an ironical flavour,
but he was not smiling.

' What happened to cause the loss?'

' We met with an upset in the Vorder
Rhein,' he said indifferently. ' It might have
been rather an ugly business; and, as it was,
the unlucky driver came in for a broken leg.'

' But you were neither of you hurt?'

' Nothing to speak of. Are you here
alone?'

' Yes. Nan and Susan are staying with

my married sister, and my father and mother are at home, doing Darby and Joan quite by themselves.'

' Happy people !'

' Do you think so ? I can't imagine any person who would like it less than you— except one,' she added with a laugh.

' Who is the exception, pray ?' he asked with a quick glance.

' Oh, I don't venture on names. But I think it rather a dangerous experiment for the generality of people.   Don't you ?'

' As to that, most steps in life are necessarily experiments, and most experiments are dangerous, the moral of which axiom may be summed up in the fact that we have often to make the best of a bad matter.'

' Or to be less hasty over our experiments,' said Elizabeth coolly.

She was thinking of Millicent, and she had never been able to forgive Sir Henry, so that she hoped her words stung. He gave no sign, however, if this were the case. Two or three others came into the hall.

'Who is that?'

'The girl or the man?'

'The man I imagine we both know—Basil Gray. The girl?'

'Miss Church—Miss Lizzie Church, an American heiress.'

'They're all heiresses, aren't they? All, at any rate, who show upon the English horizon.'

He seemed to be absolutely indifferent to Basil Gray's appearance, and Elizabeth could not see that he threw one glance in the direction of his wife, or noticed his cousin's effusive greeting, of which she had missed nothing. Jealousy had her in his gripe.

'Joan is looking very well,' she said.

He made no answer.

'But altered—so completely altered! I don't think that anyone who had not seen her since that night when we all dined with Millicent would recognise her. I never saw such a change. I dare say that you scarcely perceive it.'

'Yes,' he returned quietly, 'I perceive it.'

'Then,' Elizabeth went on, 'Nan and I amused ourselves by calling her our country cousin; certainly no name could be much more inappropriate now.'

He was silent again, and at this moment old Mr. Dunmore, a member of Parliament, who had been greatly delighted at hearing of Sir Henry's arrival, made his way into the corner and fastened upon him with joy. He was very fat and very prosy, and Elizabeth hastily jumped up. But when at intervals she glanced towards that corner of the hall, she saw Sir Henry's powerful face touched with grave interest of listening, as if he were in congenial company. Joan and Basil Gray were at a little distance, near the piano, Lady Selina's two small boys were playing with a big retriever, and Miss Church was entertaining herself and the rest of the party at the same time.

'Oh, I think Chester is the most perfectly lovely old town !' she was announcing ; 'and I never saw anything like you English people. You think all the world of yourselves, and yet you never can say it straight out. " Yes, my dear, it's a nice old place, and you'll very likely consider the Rows rather interesting,"' she went on, so exactly mimicking Mrs. Dunmore that everyone laughed. 'Why, I couldn't tear myself away. I wanted to go every bit of the way round the walls, and Mr. Gray offered to go with me ; but Mrs. Dunmore wouldn't let me—she was so very severe—she said it wasn't proper. I'm getting to know quite a number of things that you don't call proper in England.'

'Poor Lizzie ! What did you do ?' asked Lady Selina.

'Why, as we weren't allowed to go on the walls, I got Mr. Gray to go with me to Bollond's, and we bought a wedding-cake.'

'Bought a wedding-cake ? Who for ?'

' For myself, of course.'

' But—but we never heard you were going to be married,' said Mr. James Dunmore, in bewilderment.

' Good gracious, I'm not going to be married !'

' Then what did you get it for ?' demanded Lady Selina, as soon as she could speak.

' Why, to eat. What's the good of it except to eat ? It's coming here, and everybody can have as much as they like—not those horrid, shabby little bits they give you at weddings. Mr. Gray likes it just as much as I do, and he quite agrees with me that one ought to taste it beforehand, so as to know where one is. I should think I wasn't going to Chester without doing that.'

It was quite clear that Mr. James Dunmore's amazement was not lost upon this young lady, and that she greatly enjoyed exciting it, particularly when it was due to what he evidently regarded as a wicked waste of money. She went on relating several instances of immense and reckless prodigality on her own part and that of others, until he was roused to remonstrance.

' Well, if one has the money one has got to spend it somehow,' she returned, with extreme carelessness.

' Mr. Dunmore won't agree with you there,' Lady Selina said wickedly. ' How on earth do you get so much money ?'

' Oh, I don't know—mother just sends it to me, don't you know ? That's your great English expression. Every girl I speak to says "don't you know ?" twenty times in a minute. I'm going to take it back with me to America. Well, mother sends it to me. She sent me a hundred pounds this morning. I don't want it ; but she will go on sending, so I've got to spend it, don't you know ?'

' But not to waste it,' said Mr. Dunmore with decision.

' Waste it—how ?'

'On wedding-cakes, when—when you are not going to be married.'

'It would be a great deal more wasted if I were,' she retorted, 'and I don't see it's more waste than your cigars. You needn't eat it, anyway.'

Lancaster perceived that evening that his wife was in better spirits than she had been since their marriage. She danced untiringly, and made no secret of her preference for Basil Gray as a partner. But Elizabeth Ashton, who was also watching, fancied that his charm for her lay rather as a dancer than as anything else; they suited each other perfectly, and 'that contents her,' reflected the elder girl; 'that is all she is capable of caring for.' Several times in the course of the evening she either went and said a few words to her husband, or nodded to him with a radiant smile, and it was evident that she saw no reason why he should not be content with these little crumbs of regard;

but to him the awakening had been so rude,
the compensation offered seemed so meagre,
that he could not receive them in the light
in which it was possible she regarded them,
and his grave looks, Elizabeth believed, re-
pelled her.   If this were so, however, she
gave no sign of caring, but danced, laughed,
and was unmistakably happy.

Basil Gray's greeting of his cousin had
been quite free from rancour, and quite
unconcerned.

'Back again?' he said. 'But not in
harness yet, I suppose?—if you ever care to
be out of it, that is to say.   My mother
said you'd been down to Roehampton; she
was awfully pleased.'

'I thought my aunt looking remarkably
well, but Mary seemed thinner than ever.
She struck me as wanting a change of some
sort,' said Lancaster, doing his best to speak
cordially.

'Poor old Mary!' returned his cousin

with a laugh. 'She'll always be thin—takes everything to heart too much. Now there's Sissy—she's very fond of Sissy—but the care of the child wears her to fiddle-strings. Did my mother tell you what I'm hoping to walk into?'

'No.'

'Well, in a lucky moment, when I was pretty nearly on my last legs, I ran down to see Aunt Gray. She was stiff at first, but came round, and as good as promised to buy me old Adam's share in the Shelford Bank. He can't last long, and meanwhile they will pay me four per cent. for the money. Not a fortune, but will help a lame dog over a stile—unless I marry Miss Church.'

'Are you thinking of marrying Miss Church?'

'Yes, I am. I'm thinking of it a good deal. Unfortunately, she isn't thinking at all. If you could get me made a peer now?

But I'm afraid you don't think me a satisfactory subject ?'

' I advise you to stick to the bank,' said Sir Henry with an effort.

' Not I, thank you.   I shall have nothing to do with the bank until old Adams falls out of it.   I mean to hold on in London, drop in at your house, do small-talk for you—you big men never have any—and amuse Joan.'

Lancaster winced.   Joan !   Still, Basil was his first cousin, and he could hardly find fault with the familiarity.   But he could not keep his displeasure out of his voice.

' Joan will be much obliged.'

' Yes, I think she will,' said Basil coolly.

CHAPTER XXIV.

Day by day Lancaster, with a sort of despair, felt his wife slipping from him, and felt himself powerless to hold her. He did not know what to do. In the midst of the gay young party, brimming over with life and merriment, he knew himself, though scarcely older than they, to be as taciturn as if a high barrier of years lay between them and him. Elizabeth Ashton was the gravest, the nearest to him, and Elizabeth, he was aware, did not like him. His wife was the gayest, and — it sometimes seemed — the farthest away. There was not an amusement into which she did not eagerly fling herself; there was nothing in which he could think that she wanted him. He remained an outsider.

In this experience he was not the man to spare himself anything, or to clothe his failure with pretences. He set it all in bare nakedness before him—his contempt for the women who lived for fashion and excitement, his belief in his own faculty for reading character, his delusion, his awakening. He was to be wiser than a dozen better men, and here was his wisdom and its result. Here was his simple country girl—here! As he thought of it he laughed.

But he laughed with a resolve in his heart. He took his political life for a refuge; for if they two were to live two lives, his first love was waiting to welcome him back, and had never seemed so inviting. This he was master of, and in it he need not fear disappointment. So, farewell, foolish rosy visions of home and happiness; farewell, dreams of a young wife whose heart should lie safe in the man's strong keeping ; farewell, fancies of lives each giving what the other needed, until they reached one perfect round —for all this had been in his head two short months ago. He heard his wife's light laugh on the stairs as he thought of it, and, raising his head, caught sight of himself in one of the many mirrors—a clumsy, rugged-looking, massive man. He stared long at this image, thinking that had he been but wise enough to recognise the teaching of contrast in time, much suffering might have been spared them both. But he had been so careless of appearances that his own had not greatly struck him in this light, and, indeed, it is possible that it might not have struck him now if he had not chanced to hear a laughing remark of Joan's to Lady Selina the day after their arrival.

'Yes, I hope I shall soon succeed in making Henry presentable,' she was saying. 'I

make him have his hair cut much more
often, and I am trying to persuade him to
go to a better tailor, and——'

It was at this moment that Lancaster stepped
back from the window where he was standing.
Joan coloured a little, but he was only smiling.

'No, Joan; Lady Selina will agree with
me that one shouldn't desert old friends.
I have stuck to the same tailor too long
to change now. Besides, I flatter myself
it would break his heart.'

'Well, you might speak to him,' said his
wife, recovering herself.

Lady Selina fancied that she was a little
afraid of her husband, but fearful above all
things of admitting the feeling ; it sometimes
struck her, for she was shrewd enough, that
there was a touch of bravado in her conduct,
a defiant determination not to yield herself
to authority. But this was a mere guess.
What everyone saw and commented on, was
her indifference.

Miss Church, whose wedding-cake daily graced the luncheon-table, openly expressed her disapprobation to Basil Gray.

' Now, look there,' she said on one occasion ; ' I should think she might show him a little more respect, at any rate, and he such a distinguished man ! He's going to speak at Leeds on the twenty-ninth, and Lady Selina asked her if she meant to go, and she said, " No, certainly not." So then I put in my word. I wanted to know if he wasn't one of your best speakers, and she laughed and said she supposed so, and then I asked if she had often heard him, and she said never but once, and that wasn't this sort of thing at all. I've no patience with her. I should think she ought to be glad to walk there barefoot if she got such a chance.'

' He wasn't the husband for her,' said Gray, twisting round on the music-stool, and striking a few notes.

' I dare say you believe you would have

suited her better, and I don't say you
wouldn't.'

'I'm very much obliged to you.'

'Oh, you needn't be too grateful; it isn't
much of a compliment.'

'Well, you see, I withstood her charms.'

'Or she yours. Which was it?' asked
Lizzy innocently.

'You're too hard, Miss Church; but I'm
thick-skinned. Other charms have sent hers
out of sight—they have indeed!'

Miss Church turned and looked at him.

'Is that so? Now, I wonder how much
you men think we girls can swallow? I do
wish just for once you'd be honest and tell
me. You needn't mind, it won't make any
difference; I dare say you meant to propose
to me in the next day or two, and if you did,
it will save time and trouble if I tell you that
I shouldn't accept you. So that's comfortably
over, isn't it? and you needn't waste any more
pretty speeches on me; because, you see,

except my money, there isn't anything
beautiful about me, and Lady Lancaster's
perfectly lovely, and I know it quite well.
though I am a woman, and might be supposed
to be a fool.'

It must be owned that Basil Gray was a
little discomfited by this plain speaking. It
was true that he had intended to propose to
the heiress, and his easy hopeful vanity had
led him to think that he had a good chance of
success. The calm fashion in which she had
forestalled his intention, and pointed out its
futility, left him for once without resource,
except a stammer :

'Really, Miss Church——' he began, but
she went on without attending.

'I don't think that's any excuse for you,
though.'

'What on earth do you mean ?'

'Oh, don't you know?' she asked, facing
him again with her honest eyes. 'I mean
that you're always paying her little attentions

in a particular sort of a way. I don't think
it's very respectful to your cousin.'

'What a person you are for respect! If
my cousin's the fine sort of fellow you seem
to think him, he ought to be able to take
care of himself.'

'And I dare say he can,' she said con-
fidently. 'I wasn't thinking so much of him
as of you. He doesn't look like a man who
wanted much help from anybody.'

It will be guessed from this spirited conversation that Miss Church had been very
much impressed by Sir Henry Lancaster,
which, indeed, was the case, and she was
also of opinion that he was not sufficiently
appreciated by his wife or his cousin. But
her fearless attempt to point this out to the
latter was about as successful as such attempts
generally are, for it did no more than pique
Gray into a desire that she should discover
that he could be irresistible, while her praise
of Lancaster raised his jealousy. Moreover

he had been a little kept in order by the necessity of making love to Miss Church, and as that now appeared to be useless, nothing remained except to amuse himself.

Elizabeth was scornfully miserable. Before Joan came there had been moments when, in spite of experience, in spite of reason, she had been almost happy, when a touch from old days seemed to have reached the present, and fond hopes, which spring up quickly on soil watered with tears the instant warm sunshine falls on it, grew apace, and almost blossomed. Basil had been again the old Basil, had talked of his child, of a possible home, of many things which made her heart beat; and while she knew all the while that she was a fool to trust him, trust him she did, and was content to call herself a fool. Even when Miss Church took off his attentions, Elizabeth was not troubled. He did not love the American girl, and she made excuses for his thought of the great fortune;

so that the love-making—at which, indeed, he himself mocked—did not hurt her. Joan was different. By the intuition of love she knew that her beauty affected him ; his looks turned towards her, and she began to realize that after his own fashion he must have loved her.

It appeared, indeed, that Joan was careless as to this fact becoming patent to the world. Walking, dancing, or sitting still, Basil Gray was always at her side, and she had always a smile for him. She turned to him for whatever she wanted, and the two were on the easiest of terms.

The Dunmores had left, others had come —a girl who played the violin, and two men who sang. The weather was such that several long expeditions had been organized, and sometimes two or three of the party passed the morning, lazily enough, in a boat on the lake, or swung in the hammocks under the trees. Gradually, Lancaster had withdrawn from everything. Even had anyone wished him to join them, it would all have been unbearable to him ; the idle chatter, the frittering away the hours, was what he hated with deadly hatred. But, as it was, no one seemed to expect that he should do anything but occupy himself with his large correspondence, and, when he chose, walk out to meet the shooters. A study had been made over to him, and, the joy of work coming back to him, it cannot be said that he was unhappy. But it may also be said that he felt at times —and chiefly when he heard a young girl's voice raised merrily on the terrace outside his window—he felt a sick yearning for that vision of his which had lasted such a little while, and had been so fair while it lasted.

One day as she passed his window—for a wonder alone—a sudden impulse stirred him. She had looked in and smiled, and he started up and called her name.

'Do you want me ?' she asked, pausing.

'Yes. Come in through the small terrace door.'

When she reached the room he was standing by the window.

'He has no manners,' she thought impatiently. 'Basil would have been holding open the door.'

Yet when he began to speak there was something in his voice which had never been in Basil's.

'Where do you keep yourself all the day, Joan? I never have a sight of you.'

'Oh, I have only been about in the woods. You can't expect me'—with a touch of impatience—'to pass my days in this little den?'

'No, I don't expect that,' he said quietly; 'but is it always to be like this, Joan?'

'Like this?'

'Are we always to be as far apart—you living your life, I mine? That is hardly marriage.'

For the moment she looked startled. Then she said slowly :

' I don't think it could ever be very different, could it ? We should never be likely to care for the same things.'

' Then this,' he said, turning slightly away from her — 'this is what you expected ?'

Strangely enough, these last words of hers gave him his sharpest pang. It would have been better, a hundred times better, to have known that she, too, had had an ideal, and been disappointed in it. For a moment she hesitated.

' I—think so,' she returned. ' I—I suppose you would never be able—you know— to enjoy things as I do. I don't see how you are to begin.'

He took her hands in his and looked into her lovely eyes.

' But I could try. If you wished it, I could try, Joan,' he said eagerly.

Again she hesitated, and then, pulling away her hands, broke into a peal of laughter.

'Oh, you couldn't—you couldn't!' she cried, as soon as she could speak; 'you would never know how to set about it. It would be too comic! You don't know how absurdly old you are—for your age, I mean. Of course, you are really quite young for a man; but, then, no one would ever suppose it—they wouldn't, really! No, no; please don't think of such a thing. You're much happier here with all your heaps of papers and things. How dreadfully dry they do look! I shall fly!'

He held her back.

'Couldn't you stay for a little while?'

'Not very well. We are going out on the lake.'

'Have you written to Denningham?'

'No,' she said, pouting slightly. 'Must we accept? Two or three people from here

are going on to the Trenarrens, and that would
be much more amusing.'

'We must certainly go to Denningham,' he
said gravely. 'I should be extremely sorry,
after Lord Waterton's kind letter, to do anything which should appear like a slight. What
day will you fix ?'

' Oh, not before the thirtieth, *please.*'

He was silent for a moment.

'You know that I speak at Leeds on the
twenty-ninth ?'

'Yes, I know.'

' Joan, will you come ? It would be a great
pleasure to me to have you there, and, if that
has any influence with you, I think I should
speak better.'

Her face clouded.

' Oh, Henry !' she exclaimed piteously.

'You would not like it ?'

'I do think it would be dreadfully dull. A
political meeting !'

Lancaster drew back.

36—2

'Then you had better tell Lady Selina. She proposed going and taking a party. I always thought that was a mistake.'

But Joan was radiant again.

'Oh, do you mean that the others would be there? Of course, that would be delightful. And then what shall we do? I suppose we can't come back here?'

'We shall go direct to Denningham.'

Her husband's face was turned to the window, and his voice sounded like that of a man who had gone through severe bodily fatigue. She did not, however, notice it.

'I suppose we must,' she said unwillingly. 'Yes, yes,' as a voice was heard calling; 'I am coming!'

She was gone, and he crossed his arms upon the writing-table, and laid his head down upon them. This was the end of all his attempts—failure.

That evening the manner of their going to Leeds was eagerly discussed. It appeared that Miss Church was its prime mover and most enthusiastic supporter, and that she was in a condition of great elation at the success of her scheme. Mr. Selcombe was bored by the prospect, but too good-natured to resist his wife ; and as certain of their guests were leaving on that day, and others not coming until the first, matters were much simplified.

'Well, now, who's going, and when are we to go?' asked Lady Selina at dinner. 'Sir Henry, I hope you are tremendously flattered by being accompanied by our escort to the scene of your labours ? It takes a good deal, I assure you, to attract me to Leeds—at least, I think it must. Charlie, have I ever been to Leeds ?'

' Not to my knowledge.'

'Then I haven't. But I feel as if I had. Well, good people, when shall we go ? Who knows about trains ?'

' I am sorry to say,' said Lancaster, who

sat by her, 'that I must be there early in the day for some preliminary business; but you might come by an afternoon train, and I can order rooms for you when I telegraph for my own.'

'Mind, Sir Henry, we're not going to miss *any*thing,' said Miss Church warningly. 'I'm going for instruction, and I must have it all from beginning to end. I haven't looked forward to anything so much for I don't know how long. And you'll get us nice places? But of course you will. I expect to be made more of than ever I was in my life before.'

'I suppose Joan will go early with you?' said Lady Selina, it must be owned mischievously.

Lancaster glanced quickly—he could not help it—at his wife.

'Will you, Joan?' he asked eagerly, leaning forward.

'I? Oh no!' she said lightly. 'I should

be dreadfully in the way, and I couldn't be left in that odious place by myself. No, I shall keep with you all.'

' And who are all ?' asked Mr. Selcombe, looking round. ' You, Miss Church, and you, Selina——' He paused. ' That's about all, isn't it ?'

' Four ! We ought to make a better show than only four,' said Lady Lancaster quickly ; ' and we shall certainly want more gentlemen, in case anything happens.'

' Does anything ever happen ? What ?' demanded Lizzy Church, in high glee.

' We might be pelted.'

' Good gracious ! do you pelt ladies in England ?'

' My wife is thinking of elections,' said Lancaster quietly. ' Such a thing might accidentally happen then, but you need have no fears on this occasion. Besides, there will be plenty of people to look after you. I can't promise you anything so exciting, Miss Church.'

'I'd go like a shot if you could!' cried young Dick Hamerton. 'Anyhow, I think I'll go. There might be a chance of a lark.'

'Dick — that's five,' said Lady Selina, touching the tip of her thumb. 'Any more? Mr. Gray?'

'I think not, thank you. I don't think I can honestly support Henry's politics.'

There was an outcry, general except as to Lancaster, who made no movement of surprise.

'Why, you're not ratting, are you?' said Mr. Selcombe strongly.

'Don't know, I'm sure. Is that what you call an independent thinker? I dare say I am.'

'Hang it, man! you'd better find out.'

'Well,' said Lady Selina, interposing hastily; 'then it's all settled. We shall be five.'

'Five going, and you'll leave me there,' said Miss Church.

'Oh, Lizzy, no! We shan't have finished the bride-cake.'

'Well, now, aren't you all glad I bought it? I never had enough almond icing before; it always seemed so greedy to take as much as one wanted, though I can't see why people should be so mean about their bride-cakes. But they are.'

That evening they danced, and in the intervals of dancing Lady Lancaster and Basil Gray were sitting in the deep window-seat in the shadow of a curtain. She said at once:

'Of course you must come with us to Leeds. Why did you refuse?'

'Why?' repeated Gray, stretching his elbows back lazily. 'If you ask me, I suppose it was because that sort of thing isn't in the least my style.'

'I know that,' said Joan impatiently. 'It isn't in the least mine. Did you suppose it was?'

' Well, you see, I don't know,' in the same lazy tone. ' You've married into it.'

' That doesn't matter. It bores me awfully, or would, if I allowed myself to be bored by it ; but that's just what I am determined to make a stand against. I know Henry would like me to read his speeches, but I've had quite enough of that with papa, and so I shall take very good care not to begin. Don't you think I'm right ?'

' Don't I always think you right ?'

' Yes, you do,' said Joan, with a laugh ; ' that's one comfort ! At any rate, if you don't, you know how to pretend you do. So now I say that you're to come to Leeds. and you can't get out of the hole, because you would have to say that I was wrong.'

' Oh, special pleader !'

She started up.

' Dance, dance ! We are wasting the loveliest waltz !'

But she had not given up her purpose, for

when next she stopped it was close to Lady Selina.

'Mr. Gray has repented, and is coming with us to Leeds,' she said triumphantly; 'so now, Selina, we are six.'

She was gone, without waiting for an answer.

'Tyrant!' whispered Gray softly.

'A beneficent tyrant. Why shouldn't you come? Why shouldn't we enjoy ourselves? You are the idlest man I know, and that is what I like in you so much, because you have time to be pleasant.'

'It is easy to be pleasant—to you.'
She laughed.

'Oh, I know! You wouldn't trouble yourself much in that way if I were ugly and awkward. We quite understand each other.'

'Try as I might, I could never conceive you as even approaching to such a description, and so I shall not take the trouble to defend myself.'

' And you go with us ?—you yield ?'

' What else can I do ?   But, Joan.'

He dropped his voice.

' Yes ?'

' You forget that while all this may be amusing enough for you, it is not so entertaining for me, and you are apparently quite indifferent how much I suffer.'

She stopped dancing, and looked at him with a smile.

' Poor fellow !   I thought you could dance for ever.   Do you mean that you are out of breath ?'

' You know that is not what I mean.   You know——'   He broke off his sentence abruptly, for Joan had turned her back and was chatting unconcernedly with young Dick Hamerton.   He stared after her, and then broke into a laugh.   ' Hang it all ! I can't make her out,' he said to himself quite cheerfully.   ' She doesn't care for Henry—sometimes I think she doesn't care for anyone in the world. She's a rum mixture, and, by Jove, beautiful as she is, I don't think Henry need be envied. Still—well, I'll go and have a smoke.'

Young Hamerton, indeed, with whom Joan was now dancing, was at the summit of delight. His sisters always declared that he trod on their toes and tore their dresses, and though the accusations enraged him, he felt the dismal force of facts. But here was the lovely Lady Lancaster condescending not only to dance with him, but assuring him that she thought with a little practice and teaching he would dance very well; and, after that, what mattered his sisters' scoffs and gibes? Except Selina, they were none of them even grown up, and he would have it out with them! He was in quite a different position now, a much bigger man, counted as one of the guns when his brother-in-law went out, instead of being allowed to join the party on good-natured sufferance. He had held his own, too, and the keepers addressed him with deference. Hitherto this had been all that he had desired, but now—dancing with Lady Lancaster, encouraged, even praised, by her, he felt that he had passed beyond the reach of schoolroom mockery. So happy, indeed, was he, and so genuinely grateful, that he confided his delight and relief to Joan, and she, recognising some of those tremors from which, in their feminine form, she had suffered herself, was charmingly kind to him. Lancaster, who was not in the hall, unfortunately did not see her; unfortunately, because in her face at this moment he might have recognised the Joan of his visions.

Lady Selina, careless but good-hearted, was not well pleased with what had happened that evening. Elizabeth Ashton was going away the next day, and Lady Selina came to her room at night, and sat down before the fire for a talk.

' I wish you were going with us on this

expedition to Leeds,' she began, 'and yet I am half sorry that I ever agreed to go at all. If it were not for Lizzy, I should put a stop to it; but Lizzy has set her heart upon it, and I suppose it is better to go straight on now that things have been talked over. Still, I don't like it. I think Joan is behaving very badly.'

'What has Joan been doing?' asked Elizabeth, with a sinking of her heart.

Then Lady Selina told her.

'I knew she meant him to go; I saw her face at dinner, when he refused. But, really, she seems to have no shame; for she flirts with him in the most audacious way! And not married two months! What will she be by-and-by? Elizabeth, I really think you ought to speak to her before you go.'

'I?'

'Yes. You're her cousin, and you might tell her that if she goes on like this, she'll get herself talked about as sure as fate. I'm sure

I was thankful when old Mrs. Dunmore went away. As it was, I saw her watching her with her sharp little eyes, and you'll see if something doesn't get said.'

' I can't speak,' said Elizabeth coldly. 'And I can't pity Sir Henry, for anybody could see that she was quite unsuited to him from the first.'

' Well, yes. Still, I never expected such a development, did you ? She was very young and inexperienced, and all that, you know, but I always thought that though her head might have been turned a little—and I'm sure it was not to be wondered at, for if ever a man was a goose about his own daughter, Lord Medhurst was that man—however that might have been, I fancied she would get all right in the end ; I fancied her heart was right. But now—now, really I begin to doubt whether she has any heart at all, or only a little vain bubble of a thing in its place. You can't accuse me of being over-particular, Elizabeth, but I do think that to go on like this when she is only just married is carrying matters a little too far.'

'What does Mr. Selcombe say?' asked Elizabeth, for she had a good opinion of Mr. Selcombe's sagacity.

'Charlie? Oh, men are all alike; they can think of nothing except whether a girl is pretty or not. Charlie just laughs and says she's uncommonly good-looking, and he doesn't think there's any harm in her. I dare say there isn't, but there's a lot of silliness, which sometimes comes to the same thing, and you had really better see if you can't say something.'

'I couldn't—I couldn't, indeed!'

'Couldn't you give him a hint? You know him very well, don't you?'

'I!' cried Elizabeth, in horror. '*I* speak to Mr. Gray!'

'Oh, well, I suppose you couldn't!' Lady Selina said regretfully.

Why she should be taking all this interest
she could not have told herself; for it must
be owned that she too often contented herself
with an airy shrug of her shoulders when the
misdoings of her acquaintances were commented upon in her presence. There may
have been a little touch of political concern
as to anything which so nearly concerned Sir
Henry Lancaster—a dislike that even gossip
should find food in his wife's conduct. There
may also have been—and as Lady Selina
had a warm heart, this is, at least, as likely a
reason—a stirring of pity for the young wife,
who seemed so deliberately to be flinging
away her happiness. And, therefore, though
she would not go to the length of speaking
herself, she tried to stir up Elizabeth, and,
as we have seen, failed.

Elizabeth, indeed, would have done no
good, for she could not be just to Joan, and
she was yet more bitter against Basil. She
found refuge in bitterness—it was a relief to

her wounded pride to feel that she could blame, to imagine that she detested him. She scourged him with scorn; she said to herself a hundred times a day that now her eyes were open, now she had read him clearly; never again, it was certain, could her foolish heart creep back into its thraldom. She watched him—merely that she might pour out her indignation in burning thought. She welcomed the pain of it—because surely such pain meant healing. She turned away when she saw him coming — but her ear ached with straining for the sound of his voice.

There had been a pause after Lady Selina's last words—a pause which both employed in looking intently at the fire. Then the same speaker took up her words more decidedly.

'No, you couldn't. It would be a difficult thing for anyone to do. 'Heigho!' she yawned, and got up; 'I suppose, as usual,

matters must be left to take care of themselves. Good-night!' At the door she
paused. 'I think you had better come to
Leeds with us, after all.'

'Do you?' said Elizabeth weakly.

CHAPTER XXV.

THE meeting at Leeds was one which, among
a host of others which occupied the recess,
was held by the Government to be of considerable importance. The speakers were
chosen with care, and foremost in the
number was placed Sir Henry Lancaster,
who could always be trusted to make an
impression, to use telling arguments, and to
keep his temper. A strong man was necessary, for it was not unlikely that a hostile
spirit would make itself felt, and probably
felt unpleasantly; and a brilliant man, such
as even his enemies allowed Sir Henry to be,
might be able to improve the position of the

party to which he belonged. The ostensible object of his coming was to open a workmen's institute, and this ceremony would take place in the afternoon, while in the evening a huge mass meeting would be held in the large hall, and the most important speeches delivered there. As the time between the two meetings would be fully occupied by a private dinner given at the club, it was impossible for Lancaster personally to look after the party who were to follow him from Penniston. Mr. Selcombe, however, was quite capable of arranging everything that was necessary, and Sir Henry did not forget to speak to those in authority so as to secure sufficient seats near at hand.

He was met on his arrival by an enthusiastic number of warm supporters, as to the heartiness of whose greeting there could be no doubt, for they cheered him till they were hoarse. From the railway-station he drove direct to the institute through the busy

streets. The day was gloomy, a heavy
atmosphere brooded over the great city, and
now and then condensed itself into a cold
misty rain. Lancaster noted everything—
the state of the skies was not a matter of
indifference to the orator who held that it
affected men's minds and moods ; the faces
of the people were studied as telling him
what line would be most effective in speaking
to them ; the veriest trifles were seized upon
by his rapid intelligence, and turned to use.
Near the door of the institute a very large
crowd had taken advantage of the space to
collect, and here the cheers were mingled
with a good deal of judiciously-disposed hiss-
ing. Lancaster's face kindled at the sound.
One of the gentlemen who followed him into
the institute—a fat man, whose manner be-
trayed nervousness—turned anxiously to a
second just behind.

'Well ?' he whispered.

'He'll do—he'll fetch them. But it wouldn't

surprise me if we had warmish work to-
night.'

' Can't they be kept out ?'

' Not they.   And I tell you what : so long
as he can make himself heard, I shouldn't
wonder if he went all the better for a bit of
a row.   Looks like a man who would pull
better against the stream than along with it.'

This element of opposition was not present
at the afternoon meeting, which, consisting
entirely of invited admirers, was enthusiastic
throughout.   Sir Henry's speech was ad-
mirably suited to his hearers ; his arguments
were incisive, and his retorts upon the policy
of his adversaries striking, but, above all, his
speech was eminently characterized by downright common-sense, such as appealed forcibly
to these hard-headed men, held their attention, and evoked their heartiest cheers.
What he said was so simply put, so plain
to understand, that each man felt as if his
own thoughts had sprung into life, and were

being passed on to the world in the very words and form he would have chosen. Nothing could have been better. The speech aroused no feelings of surprise, it contained no burst of eloquence, and was only occasionally and very slightly ironical. What it did was to crystallize and present in a simple and tangible form the half-formed theories, the opinions which with many until now had never risen above the stubbornness of prejudice. It gave his hearers something to have and to hold—facts with which they might fight; and it appealed to their common-sense and moral nature rather than to their enthusiasms. Nothing could have been better, and yet one or two of those who were with him on the platform must have been disappointed, for when it was over, and the institute—smelling very much of new pitch-pine—had been emptied, and Sir Henry, looking rather bored, had been carried off to the house of his entertainer, before going to the dinner prepared for him at the club, the fat gentleman who has been described as nervous remarked to his friend :

' Well, that's over, and what do you think of it ? Excellent in matter, no doubt, but I should say lacking in fire, and it didn't strike me as so very original, after all. I felt as if I could have said it all myself.'

' Did you ?' returned his companion, who, having often suffered from being obliged to listen to the first speaker's prosy outpourings, might have been excused uttering anything more like an assent.

' Yes, I did. I agreed to every word of it ; but all that he said was as simple as A B C, and as easy to remember. I must say he might have given us something with a little more—well, a little more oratory in it. Oratory—that's what he wants. And he might expand. He was too short.'

' Do you know how long he was ?'

' No; I did not happen to time him. I imagine perhaps half an hour.'

' He spoke for exactly one hour and a quarter, and I own I was amazed when I found it out.'

' An hour and a quarter?' repeated the other, drawing out his watch. ' Impossible!'

' A fact. And when you have leisure to reconsider his speech I believe you will find that there was not one single point of importance which he did not touch upon, and with regard to which he has not left a clear impression.'

' But don't you admit that his manner is too cool to carry the people with him to-night?'

' To-night I don't know that he will use the same manner. If you want fire, it would not surprise me if you had it.'

' Not among the audience, I hope. Mrs. Higginson is bent upon going to the hall, and I'm sure I don't know whether I ought to allow it. It would be excessively disagreeable, if there *should* be a row, to have ladies in one's charge.'

'There might be inconvenience, certainly.'

'I think I will go home and tell her about Sir Henry's speech this afternoon. I don't think anyone would find any difficulty in repeating it again, that's one thing—it was so remarkably plain.'

'And he didn't see that he was paying Sir Henry the best tribute in his power,' said his companion with a smile, when he related the conversation to his son. 'If those men who heard him went away each with the substance of what he said so clear in his head that he could repeat it without difficulty, more will have been done for our side than could have been effected by a dozen outbursts of eloquence such as Higginson wants. Get away as early as you can to-night, Jim. if you hope for a place.'

'All right,' replied Jim, flourishing a stick.

' Half a dozen of us are going together, in case——'

' What ?'

' In case there are crowns to be cracked.'

' You bloodthirsty young ruffians !'

' Oh no, dad, we shan't begin. We only wish to be ready. You know yourself what's been said, and if they see we're prepared they're more likely to be civil.'

There was no doubt whatever as to the filling of the great hall Long before the time fixed for the meeting it was so crowded that great difficulty was found in keeping a few vacant places near the platform. Miss Church had flatly declared that she was not going to be relegated to the back of the platform ; she, for one, had not come all that distance to listen to a lot of talking and only look at the back of the men's heads. And, as usual, a strongly expressed desire carried the day, and the ladies from Pennis-ton, with Basil Gray and young Hamerton to look after them, were installed in one of the foremost rows.

When Lancaster came in, and while a tremendous outburst of cheering shook the hall, his eyes swiftly sought his wife. The next moment they fell upon Lady Millicent, who was sitting near Joan, and whose presence was no surprise to him, since Lord Waterton had made one of the party at the club. And then, with a square and steady look, such as carried with it an impression of force, he faced the great crowd of expectant faces and sat down.

That glance at his wife had brought him no sympathy. She was flushed, and her eyes sparkled. She liked the position, and the deference that was shown to her; she was proud of her husband; but it did not seem to cross her mind that she had anything to do for him. When he turned to her she was smiling at Basil, and though Millicent's eager interested little face was

full of response, Millicent, alas, was not
Joan.

'Isn't Sir Henry going to speak? Who's
that funny little man?' whispered Miss
Church to Lady Millicent.

'That is Sir Lucas Warner, the chairman,'
she explained. 'He has to make the first
speech, and introduce Sir Henry.'

Miss Church, dutifully bent upon receiv-
ing instruction, listened to Sir Lucas with
an attention which all Dick Hamerton's
audacious impertinences could not shake.
Elizabeth Ashton was on the other side
of Lady Millicent, as far away from Gray
as possible. She was sufficiently ashamed
of her own folly in yielding to a secret desire
to make one of the party to be disposed
to punish herself sharply, and he and she
were at opposite and extreme ends. Then,
also, there was a certain balm in finding
herself near Millicent, since, although un-
acknowledged, she was convinced that her

friend's suffering had been as deep as her own, and in her presence she did not fear the constant pricks which sometimes fretted her beyond endurance. When the chairman had finished his preliminary speech, she said, with an effort after interest :

'Now I suppose we are to have our reward.'

'Have you ever heard him ?'

'Never.'

'He looks ill,' said Millicent, and stopped suddenly.

He had begun.

Begun quietly, gravely, almost indifferently. As she had said, he looked ill, and, while the chairman was speaking, his thoughts were fastened drearily upon his wife, and his failure. It struck him that this was not a good preparation for his task, and he was conscious that he had never been so heavily weighted before an important speech ; but although he did not glance at Joan again, she was there immovably in his sight, and he could not detach his thoughts from her figure, or gather them together for use in what lay before him. For the first time in his life that he could remember, he felt nervous when he realized that while yet in this unprepared condition the moment had come in which he was called upon to speak to a sea of upturned faces. For the first time the possibility of a breakdown crossed his mind like an icy blast, and his opening sentences owed their coherence to the scarcely realized mechanical force of habit.

But as these first words passed his lips, his thoughts once more rallied, and came back to his order. He himself felt the power and charm of his wonderful voice, and there was a satisfaction in the consciousness that by its aid he could not only reach the farthest corners of the great hall, but reach them in the way he wished, losing nothing either in strain or inaudibility. As he stood there, one

man facing his thousands, the thrill of feeling
that he could touch them, move them, excite
them, swept across him ; he forgot Joan ; he
was back in his old life, and his heart leapt
up as to the call of a trumpet.

So far, all that he had said had been to
outward hearing as cool and as quiet as his
speech of the morning. His arguments and
his facts were brought calmly forward, and
used to shatter the assertions made at other
meetings by his political adversaries, and, so
far, although there had always been apparent
an element of disorder at the end of the
hall, he had been listened to with attention.
But, on a sudden, and as if in obedience to
a given signal, one of his statements was
received with a derisive storm of hooting
and laughter, so fierce that Joan turned
pale and looked behind her fearfully. Dick
Hamerton sprang up, but Gray leaned across
Lady Lancaster and pulled him down.

'Keep quiet,' he counselled. 'Don't you

see that a row is just what they want? Cheer as much as you like, only keep quiet.' Then he asked in a low voice, which only his companion could hear : ' Are you frightened, Joan ?'

' No, I don't know that I am.'

' You need not be. No harm can possibly come to you. I will see to that.'

She turned to him with an amused smile.

' Did you really suppose that I was afraid on my own account ?'

' It would not have been unnatural,' retorted Basil, flushing slightly.

She often puzzled him—at this moment her look puzzled him more than ever ; but there was no time to say more, for the cheers had fairly overwhelmed the hisses, and Sir Henry's voice was audible once again.

But with a change.

Up to now, as has been said, his manner had been calm and grave, giving his hearers the impression of reserved strength. Now it was as if the sound of opposition had awakened other powers. It was not only that his magnificent voice rose clear above the din, and at last compelled silence, but the whole man seemed transformed. His eyes kindled, his large mobile mouth expressed his thought with marvellous play, and his quiet speech rose to eloquence. He shrivelled his opponents with fiery indignation, scathed them with irony ; his words leapt out, clear, crushing, distinct, and moved the mass as if it had been one man. The enthusiasm was so intense that the men who had been introduced to try to hiss him down dared not attempt it, one or two bolder spirits having been ejected in a very summary fashion. There is always something tremendous about a vast crowd dominated by one idea. The man who can excite it is a born leader, and, so long as it lasts, there is no power in the world that is greater. When Lancaster at last paused, there was a momentary hush, and then from the mass there went up cheers that reached far down the streets outside, and seemed as if they could never be checked.

Joan, bright-eyed and triumphant, was watching her husband. She expected him to look at her; she was ready when the look came to flash back her congratulations. It had all been delightful. She had been carried away, like the rest, by a storm of such eloquence as she had never heard before, and she felt a keen pride in the knowledge that the man who possessed such a tremendous power was her husband. Where might he not climb? People were looking at her, pointing her out as his wife; it was not now her beauty which gave her interest in their eyes, but the fact that she belonged to him. She caught words on all sides, from Dick Hamerton's open-mouthed ' By Jove !' to the comment behind, ' Finest speech I ever heard.' For the first time she was ready—ready with her sympathy, her delight, and waiting eagerly for him to look at her, that she might telegraph them back to him.

He did not look.

And this was from no resentment, no desire to prove that he could do without what she had hitherto withheld. Of such pettiness Lancaster was incapable. He had simply forgotten her. She had never dreamt of the danger which lay in dissociating herself from the life which up to now had been everything to him, or that in insisting that their interests should be kept apart he might find his own sufficient for him. And at this moment they had swept back upon him with simply overwhelming force; he was once more in the thick of battle, feeling the stir of excitement and tasting its triumph.

Joan had shut herself out from it, and he did not think of her.

END OF VOL. II.

BILLING & SONS, PRINTERS, GUILDFORD.

G., C. & Co.